She* wanted *to be kissed.

Just that simple. Nothing more. Just kissed.
By Brendan, in a makeshift tent on her living
room floor.

One afternoon of messing about with three kids
and Brendan in a *faux* family scene and the part
of her that was so commitmentphobic seemed to
have taken a momentary hike.

She knew there would be consequences to a kiss.
But it didn't stop her from wanting it....

Dear Reader,

One of the nicest experiences a writer can have while working on a story is when characters take you by the hand and lead you through their journey. In *Project: Parenthood* Teagan and Brendan did exactly that.

These two could be any of us—people who live their everyday lives on a learning curve that can often be steep. Something I've learned myself as I've got older and supposedly more "mature." Brendan is one of the lucky few who knows what he wants from his life fairly early on, but takes a longer road than planned to get there. I know how that goes. And Teagan is convinced she knows what she wants from life when she's really not being honest with herself. I know how that one goes, too.

In this story it just takes one little twist of fate to lead them to a place where they can see things clearly and end up where they're supposed to be. I know I love it when things like that happen, and I hope you'll love taking the journey with them as much as I did. All I've done is tell the story they told me to tell you.

Hugs and kisses,

Trish

TRISH WYLIE
Project: Parenthood

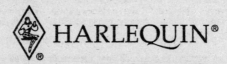

HARLEQUIN®

TORONTO • NEW YORK • LONDON
AMSTERDAM • PARIS • SYDNEY • HAMBURG
STOCKHOLM • ATHENS • TOKYO • MILAN • MADRID
PRAGUE • WARSAW • BUDAPEST • AUCKLAND

ISBN-13: 978-0-373-03922-7
ISBN-10:   0-373-03922-0

PROJECT: PARENTHOOD

First North American Publication 2006.

Trish Wylie tried various careers before eventually fulfilling her dream of writing. Years spent working in the music industry, in promotions and teaching little kids about ponies gave her plenty of opportunity to study life and the people around her. Which, in Trish's opinion, is a pretty good study course for writing! Living in Ireland, Trish balances her time between writing and horses. If you get to spend your days doing things you love, then she thinks that's not doing too badly. You can contact Trish at www.trishwylie.com

For J.H. my editor.
For encouragement and belief in me above
and beyond the call of duty....

PROLOGUE

'You look amazing. Wow. Almost like a princess.'

Teagan Delaney smiled at her younger sister's gasp of awe from the bedroom doorway. 'Why, thank you. It's amazing what you can do with three hours' preparation time. Did you get Dad's dinner done?'

Eimear nodded, her ponytail bobbing furiously before she sprawled across the cover of Teagan's bed. 'Uh-huh. I'm going to do some course revision in my room 'til you come home, though.'

It was a pretty normal thing for a seventeen-year-old to do. But Teagan knew it was also a way of hiding, 'You could watch some TV downstairs with Dad for a little while when you take a break. I'm sure he won't mind.'

Eyes the same shade of green as her own rolled towards the ceiling. 'He'll make me watch some dumb documentary. I'll just wait in my room and then you can tell me everything later.' She propped her head on an elbow. 'And you'd better. Even if I'm asleep you have to promise to wake me up.'

'I can tell you in the morning.'

'I won't sleep 'til I hear tonight!' She pouted.

Teagan raised a dark eyebrow. 'I thought you just said to wake you up?'

'I won't sleep proper.'

'Properly.'

She scowled. 'Well, I won't. You have to come tell me. I never get to go to proper dress-up parties.'

Teagan turned back to the mirror and examined her reflection. It was perfect, thanks to Eimear. Without her fashion-conscious sister she wouldn't have looked half so glamorous. Nicer jeans than normal and possibly a tad more make-up would have done the tomboy Teagan just fine. But Eimear had been more ambitious. And it had certainly paid off.

Stopping to hand out a hug of appreciation before she left the room, she felt her heart beat a little louder in her chest at the thought of what other people might think of the transformation. Hell. There was only one person she would like to impress. One person whose opinion really mattered.

She'd been spending more and more time with Brendan McNamara since he'd split up with his girlfriend at the start of the new university year.

He was the most amazing person she knew. It would be nice if he could look at her and think she was amazing too. Even if it was just for the one night.

With a promise thrown to Eimear that she would wake her, no matter how late it was, she lifted her wrap and made her way towards the stairs. As she balanced carefully on her highest ever heels, her mind turned to the only other male in her life. Who would be in the living room with his dinner on a tray and a documentary of some kind on the television.

She felt hope bubble in her chest. Surely, dressed like she was, he would take the time to tell her she looked beautiful? Just a couple of minutes to look her way and notice how much she'd grown up. That she was a woman now, and not the tomboy she'd been for most of her life.

Words of love or even a hug would be too much to hope for. But something, even a small something, would do.

He didn't even look up from his food when she made her entrance.

'I'm off now, Dad.'

'Right, then. Back by twelve.'

'Dad, it's a ball. I'll not be back 'til after one.' She tried to keep a note of pleading from her voice. 'But I'll come straight home. I promise.'

'Make sure you do.'

She waited. *Willed* him to look at her, just for a moment. But he kept on eating. 'You got money?'

'Yes.'

'Don't spend it all well.'

'I won't.' With a small sigh she scowled down at her feet and then turned to leave the room. 'I'll see you in the morning.'

'None of that bran nonsense at breakfast.'

'Fine.'

Swallowing down the lump in her throat, she turned and walked away from him. She should have known better than to even hope, shouldn't she? Years of disappointment should have taught her not to believe in any form of magic from her father. Or even from the mother who was gone.

It was just a shame she wasn't as thick-skinned as the years should have taught her to be.

Thank heavens she had a friend like Brendan. He gave her hope in the rest of the world.

Within a few hours he had put the smile back onto her face, with his easy banter, teasing tones and quiet confidence.

He was truly amazing. Around him she actually found herself feeling happy and carefree, even if reality was always in the background to remind her that life *wasn't* carefree and happy.

Brendan had been her flatmate's boyfriend when she'd met him. Which had technically made him 'safe' to get to know. There had been no danger in being friends with him because the three young women who shared the flat had had an unwritten rule about stealing guys. Not that Teagan would even have thought about it. She had more important goals than some guy's arm to dangle from.

So they'd become friends. Had almost been forced to during the times when Shannon had been late back from her part-time job, or spending longer than usual getting ready to go out for the night.

Teagan knew everything about Brendan McNamara. She knew he was determined about what he wanted from life, that one day it would definitely involve a home, with a wife and a family. He was warm and open, enthusiastic and optimistic, successful in everything he ever put his hand to. And to add to all that he was disgustingly good-looking.

Truly amazing. If almost a little too perfect.

He was *not* what Teagan would ever allow herself to fall for. Because he was a long-term, serious commitment.

And, truth be told, she had no intention of looking for anyone that serious. Not anyone who was seeking a happily ever after anyway. She'd seen up close and personal what a deep and 'meaningful' relationship could do to two people. Especially when along the line they got married, had kids and discovered that they really weren't that suited after all. Then things fell apart at the seams. And the children were the ones who paid for the mistake.

Teagan had sworn she would never allow that to happen to her. She never wanted any child to go through the upbringing she had.

Being friends with Brendan was absolutely the safest option. And their friendship mattered to her. She trusted him. Felt that he knew her well enough not to cross any line. And she needed to know the latter most of all, because he was testing her theories for life more than anyone else ever had.

The thing was, being with Brendan made her forget a lot of the things she had her future focused around. He made her wish she could believe in things like happily ever after.

So now, for one night, she was allowing herself to walk in a fairy tale. Dressed as a princess, dancing in the arms of a handsome prince. At Christmas. It really didn't get any better than that.

'You having fun?'

She smiled up at him. 'Yes. I don't think I've ever had more fun.'

He grinned a grin that made his dark blue eyes sparkle. 'You really need to get out more, you know. Too much studying makes Teagan a dull girl.'

'Oooh, go on—compliment me some more. I can take it.'

'I already told you twice that you look stunning tonight.' He swung her around in a circle that swooshed her long skirts against her ankles. 'I don't want to swell your head too much.'

She felt herself glow beneath his underhanded praise. Though the look on his face when he had first set eyes on her had been compliment enough already.

Looking down on her face, a low grumble of laughter escaped his lips as they swung closer to the edge of the dance-floor. 'I know. I'm a keeper, really.'

Yes, he was. For a brief moment she allowed herself to wonder at the kind of girl who *would* be lucky enough to keep him. And the slice of jealousy that tore through her made her feet falter for a second.

Oh, no. He was a *friend*. He could only ever be a *friend*.

'Watch the toes, kiddo.'

'Mmm, 'cos they're hard to miss.' Teagan quirked a brow at him, her eyes shining. 'You know what they say about men with large feet…'

His dark eyes widened slightly and then he leaned his head closer, dropping his voice so only she could hear. 'Large shoes?'

Laughing, they swung closer to the edge, and stopped below an archway. Then, as their gentle swaying stilled, something in Brendan's eyes changed. He examined her face for a long moment, his gaze seeming to memorise her before he spoke in the same low tone. 'You really are stunning tonight, Teagan.'

Looking back years later, Teagan would see what happened next as being one of those 'oh, no' moments. Everyone, at some point in their life, experienced at least one. She would find that out herself with time.

It was a kind of mental danger alert. The moment when a person knew that they shouldn't have allowed a particular thing to happen. It was a voice in the back of the mind yelling *Uh-oh—this could be trouble* moment. And for Teagan it came seconds too late.

While he looked at her with so much warmth in his eyes she temporarily forgot the small matter of all the goals she had set for herself in the not too distant future. And the pledge she'd made to avoid guys like him, who might touch her heart where it had never been touched before.

She just allowed herself to get caught up in the magic of the moment.

And as he smiled down at her with every spark of charm at his disposal, then let an upward glance direct her eyes to the mistletoe above them, she even forgot to breathe.

What she should have done was crack a joke or step

away. She most certainly shouldn't have stood rooted to the one spot and watched while his head descended.

She knew how big a mistake it was the minute his mouth touched hers.

Oh, no.

In that first touch of lips it was as if something she hadn't even known existed inside her woke up. It started with warmth where their mouths met, a sensual awareness of connecting with another person. Then the warmth moved from her mouth to her chest, causing her breath to catch and her heart to beat louder. Then there was the spiralling, tightening sensation low in her abdomen. All in one kiss. All in the space of a few minutes.

It frightened the life clean out of her. This was exactly what she had sworn she would never allow to happen to her. For a few brief moments she was losing control, was stepping into the abyss. But, unlike so many people who had no idea of what there could be at the bottom of that abyss, Teagan knew. She *knew*.

Heartbreak, agony, self-doubt, sacrifice. *Pain.*

She was twenty-one years old, with no experience of physical attraction on such a level. But she knew what the emotional cost was. And she wouldn't do that to either of them.

'No.' The word came out on a tortured whisper. 'You shouldn't have done that. We can't—'

'Yes, we can.' He squeezed his arms tighter around her waist. 'You had to know this was going to happen.'

She tugged back against his arms. 'I knew no such thing! We're supposed to be friends.'

'That's a good place to start.'

'No, it's a good way of gaining ammunition, is what it is. You have no idea what you'd be getting into.'

He obviously had no idea what she meant. The look on his face told her that. And in that second she knew she was right to do what she was doing. He didn't know her as well as he thought he did. That wasn't his fault. Because with Brendan she'd had her first chance to live in a land of make-believe. Someone who had led as charmed a life as he had could only believe that everyone else's life had been as easy. So it had been simple to play along.

But the very fact that it was hurting her so much to reject him only proved that she was right to do it. If she got any more involved than she already was then she might not survive. She might end up exactly like her parents.

'I can't believe you did this.' She finally managed to get free from his hold, her eyes flashing up at him as she did her best not to cry. 'You've ruined everything.'

'With one wee kiss? How have I ruined everything?' He shook his head and stepped towards her again, his eyes flickering around to see who could hear their argument, 'You're acting like some hysterical female, Teagan. Stop it.'

The condescending tone was like a slap in the face, 'How dare you?'

'Teagan—' His tone became more warning.

'Don't you Teagan me! Try finding someone who *wants* you to kiss them, Brendan. There are loads of women here who might want that from you. But I'm not one of them.' She raised her chin a very visibly stubborn inch and glared at him. 'Get over yourself.'

Without waiting for a response she turned and, like Cinderella running from the ball, fled across the room, the sound of her name in his deep voice echoing behind her.

She swore there and then that she would never see him

again. *Ever.* He could think that was immature or stupid if he wanted to. In fact he could think whatever the hell he liked.

All he had done was show her that the path she'd chosen for herself was the right one. She would *never* let anyone get to her like he just had. She would only ever have herself to look out for, pure and simple.

And they'd be selling ice cream in hell before she changed her mind again.

CHAPTER ONE

'YOU *can't* do this to me now!'

Eimear lowered her voice and blinked shimmering eyes at her. 'Teagan, I wouldn't ask if this wasn't really important. It could be make or break for us. I need this time with Mac to sort it out or we could be *through*.'

'I get that, Eimear. I do. But I can't look after them *now*.' She glanced over at the three small faces blinking at her from the doorway, guilt rising up in her throat like bile that they were having to hear her turn them away, *rejecting* them. 'Maybe next weekend some time. I have this massive deal in work and—'

'This is my life we're talking about! I can't lose him, Teagan. I really can't.'

And now she was crying. Teagan couldn't take it when Eimear cried. And she especially couldn't take it when it was happening in front of her nephew and nieces. Even though technically their mother's back was to them. Teagan really couldn't put them through any of the stuff she remembered from her own childhood. It would be too cruel.

But surely it wasn't unreasonable to have asked for a little warning? A phone call to discuss it? A text message to say they were on their way over? Not a carload of them outside of her house when she got home from work…

'Eimear—'

'Please. I'm begging you.'

It had been a long time since Teagan had really felt that Eimear needed her. Things just hadn't been the same between them over the years since Eimear's first marriage. A marriage that Teagan had felt never should have happened to begin with. She'd said so. Loudly and at length, in fact. And Eimear had never really forgiven her for it, so their relationship had changed.

But seeing Eimear so desperate now was like looking back in time. And it brought out Teagan's old need to soothe and to make things better.

Her eyes moved again to the three children. The eldest, Johnnie, was looking at her with eyes the same colour as his mother's. He almost looked as if he was examining her, sizing her up. And even while she stood contemplating how to get out of looking after them she felt as if she was falling short of his expectations.

She took a long breath. 'How long for?'

'Thank you!' Eimear engulfed her in a swift, tight hug, her tears gone. 'I knew I could rely on you.'

Teagan scowled, suddenly feeling she'd just been hood-winked. 'They'll need—'

'They have everything they need right there. It's all pretty self-explanatory. And Meggie is potty trained now, so she just needs a nappy on at night. It's a pull-on, so you'll be grand.'

She was still scowling while her sister became a hurri-cane around the room, hugging and kissing the children and moving towards the door. 'We'll only be a few days. Mac has booked some lovely country hideaway for us.'

'How will I—?'

'Thanks, Teagan. You really are a star.'

And she was gone.

Teagan blinked at the closed door. What had just happened? Not half an hour ago she'd had a bubble bath, scented candles and a glass of good Chardonnay planned for her evening. Now she was staring at three small faces that looked as bewildered as she felt.

She pinned a bright smile on her face as she approached them. But it took about thirty seconds for the smallest one to crumple.

'Oh, no, honey. Don't do that.'

And then the second one began to sniffle. Only Johnnie remained impassive.

It was Teagan's worst nightmare.

Brendan hated moving days. This time would definitely be the last one for a few dozen years if he had his way.

He lugged a box from his rental van and made his sixth trip into the house before rolling up his sleeves and heading out to repeat the trip.

At least his life wasn't as chaotic as it looked for the poor woman across the street.

She was making her third trip from the house to the car. This time with a screaming toddler in her arms. And from the way she was moving he could tell she wasn't having much fun. No sign of a dad to help out either. Maybe he'd had sense enough to head out for work earlier, before the chaos kicked in.

If it had been Brendan, he'd have relished that kind of chaos.

He shook his head. He should have bought a damn apartment in some new complex filled with single people.

People who didn't make up perfect little family units in a hive of houses filled with similar perfect family units.

Hell, he'd have been better off with a paper cut and some nice lemon juice to pour on it.

But the house *was* a good investment.

The woman leaned in through the car door and soothed the screaming child until there was silence. Then, running her hands back through her dark hair to tame it, she closed the door and started around to the driver's side. But halfway around the car she stopped, and there was a frustrated scream and a stamp of one high heel. Her hands rose for a moment and then dropped to her sides. 'No, not this morning! Don't do this to me!'

He stepped away from the van and looked where she was looking. A flat tyre. That sucked.

Well, he shrugged to himself, that was one way to get to meet the neighbours. And Lord knew she looked as if she could do with being rescued.

So he did the decent thing and jogged across the street. 'Hi. Do you need a hand?'

She jumped when he spoke, and swung to face him, her hair swinging across her face. 'I have a flat tyre.'

Brendan looked down at the offending object and nodded wisely. 'Yep, I'd say you do, all right.'

'I can't fix a flat tyre in this outfit.' There was a brief pause while she joined him in looking at the tyre. Then she took a breath and her voice changed. 'I don't suppose I could possibly ask you—?'

The male in him noted the shift in her vocal tone immediately. How it had changed from annoyed to beguiling in the space of one sentence. She was trying to flirt with him to get him to change the tyre. Typical woman. Obviously some ditzy housewife who had never learned how to change a tyre because her husband always did it for her.

He smiled and looked at her as she brushed her hair back from her face. And his breath caught.

'Teagan.'

Her eyes flickered up to meet his, then widened. 'Brendan.'

Blond brows quirked at the guarded way she said his name. He tried a wider smile. 'Well, this is a surprise.'

'What are you doing here?'

'I'm moving in across the road.'

'You bought the house across from me?' Her eyes moved to look at the half-unloaded van. 'When did that happen?'

'Got the keys the day before yesterday. I have to say if I'd been given a list of people I might bump into when I got here—'

'Mine would have been the last?' Her chin rose as she looked back at him, a small, tight smile on her lips. 'That's nice.'

Her cool stare brought his back up. Okay, so she was having a bad morning—obviously—but that really was no excuse to be rude. After all, he'd come over to *help*.

'Well, it's been a while.' He folded his arms across his broad chest and nodded.

'Yes, it has.'

He made another attempt at lightening the mood. Not that she really deserved it. One long finger pointed towards the car, where at least the crying hadn't started up again. 'About three of those ago, apparently.'

Teagan snorted out a brief laugh. 'Oh, they're not mine. They're my sister's kids.'

'You stole them?'

The smile she gave him was a little more relaxed. 'Nope. Why would a person do that, exactly?'

'Well, they're cute.' He waved through the window.

'Yes, they are that.' She waved herself, and was rewarded by three smiles. 'But they're also really hard work.'

'I'd heard that rumour.'

She glanced at him in the reflection of the glass, seemed to take a moment or two to think and then asked, 'Look, I'm sorry to ask you this, but is there any chance you *could* give me a hand with the tyre? I'm going to be really late to work at this rate.'

'You're taking them with you to work?'

'No.' She laughed again. 'There's a daycare centre nearby, and they've said they can take them today for me to help out. After that I'm on my own.'

Brendan took a breath as he turned to look at her. He blinked as he thought, his eyes moving over her profile while his mind remembered what she'd looked like the last time he had seen her. Nine years hadn't done her any harm. She looked great, if a little on the harassed side.

When she turned her face to his she blinked up at him with her large green eyes and he remembered more about the last time he had seen her. The night he had kissed her and she'd told him to get over himself before she ran. He'd never had a chance to see her again, to talk it out. She'd given him no choice.

And now she was his neighbour. Well...

He cleared his throat. 'I'll help with the tyre. No problem. It's what I came over here to do.'

There was a brief pause, then, 'Thanks.'

Another smile was attempted. 'You're welcome.'

Teagan hesitated for a brief moment. Then she answered the smile with one of her own. After all, he was being helpful.

She followed him around as he pulled the spare wheel from the boot and gathered the tools he needed. It gave her a few moments to think of some conversation to make. After all, a big part of her work every day was talking to people. It shouldn't be so difficult.

But all she could think of was, *Well, hell—of all the people!*

'So.' His voice sounded out from her knee height. 'No kids of your own, then?'

'No, no kids of my own.' For some completely unknown reason she felt she had to justify that. 'I'm too busy with my career.'

'Not for as long as you have these three, you're not.'

Well, thank you, Brendan, for stating the obvious. She scowled at his back as he finished jacking up the car and reached for the wrench. 'No, the busy part is still there. This wasn't a booked visit.'

His voice came out with a slight grunt as he worked on the first wheelnut. 'How are you going to manage, then? Will your husband help?'

Subtle one.

'I'm too busy with my career for a husband.'

'You must be doing great in work, then.'

'As a matter of fact I am. Thanks.' Her scowl promoted itself to a frown.

He nodded as he freed the last nut and wrenched the tyre off. 'Well, good for you.'

If she'd been a dog she'd have growled at him. In the space of a few sentences he'd made her feel as if the years since she'd parted company with him had been achievement-free. Just because his goals were different from hers, it didn't mean hers were any less fulfilling!

After all, she owned her house—along with the bank. She almost completely owned her car. Her bank balance was healthy enough to allow a shopping spree at least once a month, and she paid every one of her bills before the ink turned red. She thought she was doing pretty well for someone her age.

Who was he to waltz in and criticise?

'I suppose you're moving a nice wee wife and twelve kids in across the road, then?'

He rose and turned round, lifting the spare tyre with one hand as he grinned at her. 'Nope. Just me.'

Damn it, he'd caught her, hadn't he? He hadn't been trying to criticise her life; he'd been fishing for information. And he'd got it. And now he was grinning at her with a sparkle in his eyes that said, *Gotcha.*

Teagan shook her head with a small smile of resignation. She should have remembered how smart he was. Lord alone knew she was remembering plenty of other things while he kept on looking at her like that.

Still grinning, he turned round and popped the tyre into place, then reached a large hand out for the nuts. 'I could help if you're stuck.'

Like hell. 'I can manage. Thanks.'

'Well, if you're stuck.' He tightened the last nuts and then stood up, wiping his hands carelessly along the sides of his jeans before he lifted the flat. As he walked past her he glanced from the corner of his eye. 'I'm great with kids. I have dozens of nieces and nephews, so I've had loads of practice.'

Well, bully for him. Though for the briefest moment she allowed herself to wonder why he hadn't had any of his own. What had happened to *his* great plan for life? But she couldn't wonder about that kind of thing. Because wondering would lead to questioning. And questioning would lead to a friendship of some kind. Which would be a massive mistake.

She was mature enough to know that *now.*

'Thanks.' She straightened her hair again, then glanced at her watch as he stowed away the tyre. 'But, really, we'll be fine.'

Brendan closed the boot and studied her for a long time, his dark blond lashes blinking slowly. Then he merely shrugged his broad shoulders and pushed his hands into his pockets. 'Well, you know where I am.'

Indeed she did. But she would need to be in critical condition before she'd follow the broad shoulders that swayed as he walked back across the road.

C-r-i-t-i-c-a-l.

CHAPTER TWO

CRITICAL didn't kick in until just before she was due to leave the office to collect the children. That was when she got word that the meeting with potentially her biggest ever clients had been brought up a few days, and she had a presentation that wasn't even halfway done.

The headache started then.

At the daycare centre no amount of pleading or bribery would get the children booked in again. They were full to the gills as it was, and it was only because one family had been on holiday that they'd had space for one day.

Her head was pounding by the time she got to the local supermarket.

'I want fish fingers!'

'No, chicken nuggets!

'Fish fingers!'

'Nuggets!'

'If you two don't stop this minute you're both getting cauliflower and nothing else.' She negotiated her way around an end-of-aisle display, missing toppling a pyramid of washing powder boxes by inches.

She'd had dozens of trollies to pick from, and had still managed to pick the one with the dodgy wheel. Someone somewhere really had it in for her.

Katie pulled a face. Teagan stopped the trolley at the top of the cereal aisle and raised an eyebrow at her. 'You don't love cauliflower, Katie?'

The five-year-old held her arms around her waist and pretended to gag. Which made Teagan laugh. She was better laughing, she guessed. Otherwise she would have to stand and weep in public.

'Fish fingers.' Katie nodded furiously, then took a moment to think and added, 'Please?'

'Please certainly helps.' Teagan began to push the trolley again. 'Tell you what, let's do cereal first, and then we can decide what we're having for dinner.'

It was after nearly fifteen minutes of debate on nutritional value versus free gift in box when Brendan appeared around the corner with a basket.

'Aw, hell.' Teagan looked down at Meghan's smiling face.

'You said a bad thing!'

'I'm sorry, Katie.' She pinned a smile on her face as Brendan approached. 'Hello, again.'

'I'm not stalking you, if that's what you think.'

The thought had occurred. 'It's the closest supermarket.'

Katie tugged on his arm. 'You fixed the wheel, didn't you?'

'Yes, that was me.' He hunkered down and smiled broadly at her. 'You getting cereal? I like those ones too.'

'You get a book with them.' Katie hugged the box.

'And about a zillion preservatives,' Teagan cut in.

'They'll help her live longer.'

'No, they won't.' Teagan scowled down at him. 'Something with bran in it would be much healthier.'

Brendan made a similar gagging face to the one Katie had made during the cauliflower discussion and Katie giggled at him. 'Yuck.'

Leaning down towards his ear, Teagan snapped, 'Not helping.'

She stood up abruptly as he rose to his feet, felt herself get shy as he examined her face. 'You look wrecked. Tough day?'

'You have no idea.' She caved on the cereal with the book, soothing her conscience by at least believing that reading was educational, and vowing to balance it up by adding in some porridge oats. She'd worry about negotiations later. 'And it's only getting worse.'

Falling into step beside her, he reached a hand out and grabbed a box. 'Worse how?'

With no idea whatsoever why she was doing it, Teagan started to spill her problems. 'The deal I'm working on has been moved up, and I have this huge presentation to do in two days.'

Brendan nodded, adding more to his basket as they rounded the corner. 'And you have the kids at the same time?'

'Yes. And the daycare centre can't take them.'

'So, you'd say you were stuck, then?'

She stopped her trolley by the low refrigerators and glared at him. 'I have a list of childminders to call when I get home.'

'And if they can't take them at short notice?'

Then she was in big trouble. Blinking at his calm face, she felt the headache thump harder at her temples. If it had been anyone else on the entire planet...

'Then I'll have to see if the meeting can be put back a couple of days.' She just about managed to hide a grimace as she reached for frozen fish fingers and chicken nuggets.

Brendan stood silently until she looked back at him. 'Did your sister understand how busy you are in work right now?'

She kept her face hidden as she examined the contents of the fridge. 'She has some stuff that she has to deal with right now. It's important.'

He watched as she aimed a brief smile at him.

'Not cauliflower, Auntie Teagan.'

'It's good for us, Katie.'

'But it tastes yucky.'

'We'll put cheese sauce on it and it'll be grand.' She ruffled Katie's hair and then glanced at Brendan from beneath her lashes. 'I better go get this lot fed.'

'Sure.' He nodded, then waited to speak again as she started to force her wobbly trolley away from him. 'But remember the offer of help is still there if you need it, Teagan. Really.'

They couldn't change the meeting. And none of the child-minders she'd been given numbers for had space for all three children. Which would mean splitting them up. Which Teagan couldn't do. She had accepted responsibility for them and that was that.

So she had no choice but to bite the bullet and ask for help. From Brendan. Just for one day.

And he didn't even take a second to be smug about it when he came to the house the next day. Which made her feel worse. She so didn't want him to be around. *Seriously.*

Then and there Teagan decided it was time to track her sister down. It wasn't that she didn't want her nephew and nieces to stay. She did. It would be nice to spend more time with them. Really.

Just not right smack-bang in the middle of a big work deal.

When she got home Brendan had the world under control. Nothing appeared to have got stained, smeared or smashed since she'd left. And that in itself was a miracle she hadn't managed in the last forty-eight hours.

She sighed as she sat down at the counter in the kitchen, and smiled at the coffee he handed her.

'It's official, just so you know. I'm going to kill her when I get her.'

Harsh words. But for a split second Teagan honestly meant them. Her responsibility for her younger sister's problems should long since have ended. Somewhere around the time they both grew up and left the small hell they'd called home.

Brendan smiled from the other side of the room, 'Couldn't get through to your sister, I take it?'

'Good guess.' She managed a small smile in return, 'It's not that I don't want them. It's just that I can't manage this right now.'

'Yes, you can.' His all too familiar deeply male voice sounded firm. 'You don't have a choice.'

'Of course I have a choice. I can track her down and she can take them home!'

'But that's just it. You can't, can you?' His fair eyebrow raised a notch as he stared at her with eyes so dark a blue that from across the room they were almost black. 'Where else can they go 'til you find her?'

She glared across at him. To add to her sister's list of transgressions she now had the fact that she was being forced to spend time with the one man she'd spent nine years avoiding.

Up until he'd reappeared she'd managed to live by the 'out of sight out of mind' rule. Hadn't ever bumped into him at a party, or made the mistake of attending any re-union-type thing he might have been at.

Now, thanks to her sister, she had no choice but to accept his help. Which had brought him into her house and *directly* into her line of vision. Up close and personal.

The best-laid plans...

'Teagan?' His voice sounded again when she went silent.

'Sorry.' She scowled down into her coffee mug and tried to find answers there. 'I can't keep looking after three little kids under ten. Not right now. And I can't keep imposing on you either. I was only supposed to have them for a few days, and this contract in work wasn't due to finalise 'til next week.'

'It's no big deal. I don't mind.'

When she looked up again he was studying her, his eyes as warm as his voice was reassuring.

It was unnerving as all hell. 'You may not, but I do.'

'You can't want to see them in the care of someone you don't know? Not really.'

She scowled at his statement, admitting inwardly that that was probably the reason she got a headache every time she spoke to someone about childcare or daycare. It just didn't sit well on her.

What she *wanted* was for her sister to get herself home so that Teagan herself could have her life back. She would even offer to babysit a night or two, so that Eimear and Mac could have time alone, and she'd reschedule for them to stay. That would be fair, wouldn't it? And it would ease her guilt at not being able to help somewhat. Well, a little anyway.

It was kind of a moot point right that minute, though. She sighed. 'I can't bring them with me to the office. If I mess up this contract…' The words trailed off.

Despite the serious tone of her statement, Brendan's eyes sparkled with amusement. With her scowl as a response, he cleared his throat and forced a calm look on his face. 'You're right. Having seen what they can do to a living room in one afternoon, I guess the office is probably *not* a good idea mid-presentation.'

'Cream was a practical colour for a suite when I lived here *alone*.' She thought nostalgically of the days when all the creams and beiges of her modern interior had looked pristine. They couldn't have spilt something on something darker, where it wouldn't have shown, could they?

A small chuckle escaped. 'Thank the Lord for cushions, though. They can cover any flavour fruit juice. Even blackcurrant.'

Teagan glared. 'I'm glad you find this so amusing.'

'Aw, c'mon—you can barely see the stains when the cushions are in the right places. I always knew there had to be some use for throw cushions.' He continued to smile, adding with a shrug, 'They're such a girl thing.'

'*I* still know the stains are there.' She did her best to hide a smile of amusement. Though at the time it had happened she hadn't been so amused. She'd worked damn hard to have her lovely home lovely, spent hours poring over catalogues and wandering around furniture stores. Making things kid-proof had never once been a consideration in any of her purchases.

Pushing his large frame away from the edge of a granite counter-top, Brendan walked the two paces necessary to stand right in front of her, his voice silken. 'They need you.'

'I'm not their mother, though. Their mother should be here.' She tried really hard not to notice how close he was, or how he made words sound so seductive. Her eyes flickered up to his face. Was it possible for someone to look better under close inspection than they did from a distance? Even after nine years? Lord alone knew if she stood that close to her *own* reflection she'd find flaws. Plenty of them. And every blasted one of them a reminder that she wasn't twenty-one any more.

With a swallow she forced herself to stare at a dark button on the front of his shirt. Buttons were nice, safe things to look at. She would just focus on the button while she forced herself to find some miraculous solution to her dilemma. Reasoning to herself that while focusing on the button she wouldn't get distracted by looking into deeply blue eyes. Even when she knew they were still looking at her.

'No, you're not their mother.' He waited patiently until his silence, and his close proximity, forced her eyes to tilt up to meet his again. 'But they need you to be a substitute for them right now. You don't really have a choice, do you?'

'I'm aware of that, thank you.'

'Then you just have to manage. You'll be grand.'

He made it sound so simple. How could he know? It wasn't as if she'd ever explained to him the life choice she'd made such a long time ago. A choice that most certainly didn't involve three children running around to shatter her solitude. It didn't involve responsibility for *any* other life. Even one as small as a cat or a goldfish. No baggage. Eimear was supposed to have grown up enough so that she wasn't Teagan's responsibility any more. So that Teagan just had herself to look out for. And there were times when that was tough enough on its own.

She shouldn't have to do this kind of thing any more. It just wasn't fair. The petulant thought brought a frown to her face. Damn it. Now she was going to huff like a teenager too? That was great—just fabulous.

He watched her scowl for a few seconds, then turned his face from hers as he tucked his hands into the pockets of his worn jeans. 'I've told you I'll help out where I can.' He glanced back at her face. 'And I mean that. I'll not see you stuck.'

'I know. You've said.' She swallowed down a bubble of frustration. He just always had been such a nice guy, hadn't he? And the simple truth was he was better with the children than she was—which made her even more resentful of his presence than she already was. 'But this really isn't your problem. It's mine. I really don't need you to feel you have to hop over here to rescue me every time there's a crisis.'

'Every guy likes to play the knight in shining armour now and again.' He flashed a grin at her while ignoring her petulant tone. 'You just happen to be the nearest damsel, is all.'

Teagan hated the idea of being seen as a damsel in distress. So much for all her years trying to be a strong and independent career girl. Capable and self-sufficient. All it took was something really heavy round her house, or her nemesis of something *electrical*, and she was as much use as a chocolate kettle.

But Brendan had to have work of his own to do—things that took up his time. She swallowed as she thought, *Dates to occupy him.*

She watched with slightly narrowed eyes as he turned, removed a hand from his pocket to rescue his mug and walked the two paces it took for him to get to the sink to rinse it out. Somewhere in her mind it occurred to her that everyone else took a lot longer to walk around her open-plan kitchen. But Brendan was so damned tall that he seemed to get everywhere in two long, confident steps. She'd forgotten over the years just how tall he was.

He certainly was way head and shoulders above her shoeless five foot seven. When he was around she had always had moments where she felt feminine. Maybe even a little small and damselish.

'So, what are you going to do if you won't accept some help?'

Good question.

'I don't know.' She frowned again as the words came out all small and helpless. This really had to stop. 'But I'm going to have to think of something until I can track down Eimear.'

'And you've definitely tried everywhere?'

She'd told him as much when she'd rung to check on the children during the day, so the question brought her back up again.

'No, I only rang the once and then gave up.' Raising her hands to her hips, she tilted her head and stared at his back with a deadpan expression.

The sarcasm rolled right over him. 'What about her friends?'

She sighed a resigned sigh. What was the point in being stroppy with him after all? It was hardly his fault. 'No help. They only know that Mac took her on a romantic break somewhere on the Ring of Kerry.'

'Somewhere that doesn't have a phone so she could check on her kids?'

Which, had Teagan had her wits about her, she could have cured by taking the damn hotel details. Not that she'd thought about it while she was being so deftly hoodwinked. 'They need some time alone.'

Brendan shook his head. 'I don't understand people like that.'

He wouldn't, would he? Not this guy who had the kind of simple, easy, charmed existence that Teagan herself had only ever seen at the movies. He couldn't possibly understand why Eimear would be so desperate to save her second marriage if it was in trouble. If he ever got round to getting married it would no doubt be roses and violins the whole damn time.

A bubble of anger grew in her stomach. He knew nothing. She'd bet that nothing more troublesome than running out of milk had ever happened in his life. Not that she'd taken the time to ask since they'd been thrown into each other's paths again. It was really none of her business after all.

With his cup rinsed and set on the drainer, he turned and looked back at her face. He went silent for a moment when he saw the spark of anger in her eyes. Even after their years apart he still knew the warning signs of an impending argument. She was obviously as angry at her sister as he would have been, given the same circumstances, but she refused to hear a bad word spoken about her.

With a shrug, he let it drop. 'Well, you know where I am if you need a hand.'

Oh, she *knew*, all right. Right across the street. Right under her nose. To remind her every day of all the reasons she had to stay well away from him. Especially if there was ever any mistletoe in sight. Teagan had the memory of an elephant.

'Thanks for looking after them today.'

'No problem.' He frowned for a second, deep in thought, poised on the balls of his feet as if he might step forward again. Then he simply smiled a small smile and walked the two paces it took for him to get to her back door. 'I have some work to clear up at home tomorrow, so I'll be around if you need a hand.'

'Okay. Thanks again.' Though even as she said the words she knew she would do everything in her power to make sure she didn't have to make that call.

After the door closed behind him, she stood in the same place for a long while. The house was silent, bar the background noise from the television in her front room. If it hadn't been for that noise to remind her she wasn't alone she might have allowed herself to wallow in the moment of loneliness she felt.

But it wasn't because of *him*, she reminded herself. It was just the way she'd probably always felt but had never really allowed herself to acknowledge. It was an emptiness inside that she'd taken years to control and to bury—even from herself, it seemed.

Part of her truly hated him for the fact that he had reminded her it was there. That it might have been well hidden but it hadn't gone away. Maybe never would.

She wasn't the only one who fought it, though, she guessed.

Although right at that moment she may have wanted to kill her sister for taking this trip of hers, and inconvenient timing as it was, she couldn't hate her for it. Because she understood.

Eimear was probably fighting her own version of that hollowness, and having her children obviously wasn't enough on its own. She wanted the whole shebang—wanted a man by her side, to be made to feel loved and safe. While Teagan had chosen to find the solution in her career and a modicum of financial security.

Teagan didn't doubt for a second that she would be back soon. Eimear hadn't abandoned her children; she'd just set them to one side while she tried to fix her second attempt at marriage.

Teagan herself would never have set her own children to one side for a man, moot point though that was. She'd made her choices. She was the stronger one of the two of them—the one who got on with it, alone. As she'd just have to get on with it this time.

She'd just have to find a way to do it without Brendan McNamara's help. She didn't need a constant reminder of how close she could have come to being like her sister in seeking happiness through some guy. Even when that guy's presence still stirred up a memory in her that she'd never really been able to shift.

No, she would *never* allow herself to rely on someone

else for her own happiness. Could never expect to find love as it was described in the movies. Because it just didn't exist. Teagan knew that, even if Eimear didn't.

But then Teagan remembered more than her little sister. She'd made sure of that. It was her job to do everything she could to ensure Eimear was happy.

If that meant playing at being Mummy then that was what she would do. Other women coped, balancing careers with families.

Teagan was a mature, capable woman. She could deal with problems when they arose. Could manage her time.

It was only for a couple more days. Eimear had said a few days. And she'd survived two already.

She'd just have to find a way to survive another two. *Without* Brendan McNamara.

CHAPTER THREE

BRENDAN smiled through his window as he watched her bundle the children out through her door and into her car.

She looked harassed again. Sleek, shoulder-length dark hair flying into her face as she moved from car door to car door. Even the movements of her slight figure were jerky, hurried, while she brushed at her hair with an irritated hand.

His smile grew. Thing was, even from across the street he could see that that ruffled-round-the-edges look suited her. It was sexy. It reminded him of how sexy she'd been at twenty-one. Though he'd bet serious money she wouldn't believe him if he told her.

Not that he was likely to.

He wasn't going to even allow himself to touch on the subject of how she'd looked back then. Even Shannon, with her cover-girl blonde looks, hadn't affected him the way that Teagan could with one flick of her long dark hair or a flash of dimples when she smiled. She'd been tough to forget.

But she was determined to do without his help. Something he should have been happy about. If only from a work point of view. And it wasn't as if she'd shown any real enthusiasm to spend a great amount of time in his company since he'd moved in across the road from her.

That should have been enough of a hint for him to leave it alone. But somehow all it did was make her more interesting to him.

Maybe it was just the thrill of the chase? After all, he hadn't had to do that much chasing until he'd met Teagan Delaney. And when he'd finally made his move on her all those years ago she'd run. Literally miles away. As if her pretty little behind was on fire.

He swung back and forth on the leather chair in his home office while he let the memory of that one kiss seep into his mind. Not for the first time either. It was almost as if seeing her had opened a well of memories he'd shut away.

It had been one hell of a kiss—one he'd gladly have repeated. And he'd thought about repeating it way, way too much, for months afterwards.

But alongside the memory of that one kiss was the memory of when she'd opened her eyes and looked at him with such an expression of anguish that it had literally knocked him back on his heels.

It had been as if that one sweet, softly warm kiss had torn her heart from her chest.

Some guy somewhere had done a real number on her, hadn't he? How come he hadn't known that?

He sighed. It wasn't his problem now. Well, that was what he kept on telling himself. Women with baggage just weren't his style. They were too much work for someone who'd just got out of one big mistake and had baggage enough of his own, thanks very much.

He really should have been backpedalling like crazy to keep away from *Ms* Teagan Delaney.

But he wasn't. Instead he was volunteering every five minutes to help her out, when she would quite obviously rather chew off her own arm.

It was quite pathetic, really. And enough was enough.

What he should be doing was going straight out to pursue someone less complicated. Or a string of someone elses—with less history involved, of course. A series of flings to fill in the time; that was what was needed to take his mind off his new neighbour. Nothing else.

His focus was drawn back to the window as her car pulled out into the street and disappeared. He then watched with widening eyes as a second later her front door opened and a small figure appeared.

She'd left one behind?

With a shake of his head he got up from his chair, grabbed his keys and jogged across the street. *Again.*

This time definitely had to be the last time.

'Hey there, Johnnie.'

Johnnie looked up at him, blinked a couple of times and then answered, 'Hey.' As if nothing in the world was wrong.

'Your Aunt Teagan was in a bit of a hurry this morning, I take it?' He smiled.

'S'pose.'

'I bet she'll be back in a minute.'

Johnnie shrugged.

Brendan glanced up the street and then looked back at the house. 'I don't suppose you left the door open?'

The boy shook his head.

'Didn't think so.' They both stood silently, and then Brendan turned round and sat down on the stone step, 'Well, I guess we better wait for her, then. I'm sure she'll be right back.'

The boy thought for a moment, and then sat down beside him. And they sat. And then they sat some more. *In silence.*

Brendan told himself he was okay with that. Being quiet

was fine with him. But after a couple of minutes he glanced sidewards. 'So, how you doing?'

'Okay.'

'Aunt Teagan looking after you?'

'She's tryin'.'

Brendan nodded. 'That's good, then.'

He honestly thought he was going to have to discuss the weather with an eight-year-old when Johnnie announced, 'She doesn't have no kids of her own.'

'No, she doesn't.'

'I don't think she likes kids much.'

'Don't you?' He turned his body towards the child, curious to hear his thought process. 'How come?'

'She puts us to bed awful early.' Another shrug and he continued staring forwards. 'I think it's so she don't have to play with us.'

Brendan frowned, his mind trying to translate the reasoning of a child into the reasoning of an adult. 'How early is early?'

'Eight o'clock.'

He didn't think that was all that early. 'What time does your mum let you stay up 'til?'

Another shrug. 'I sometimes get to stay up 'til ten when there's no school.'

Which seemed late to Brendan. 'Don't you get tired?'

'We sleep in.'

'What about when you *have* school?'

The question was greeted with yet another shrug, and Brendan shook his head a barely perceptible amount. The thing was he already knew that Johnnie was the talkative one of the three.

There was the sound of an approaching car in the distance, and then Teagan reappeared.

'See—there she is.'

They stood up in unison as the car parked in the driveway.

'I thought I told you to get in the car.'

'Whoa, one minute.' Brendan frowned at her tone. 'Don't take it out on the kid 'cos you can't count heads.'

Teagan's eye's sparked angrily at him. 'This is none of your business.'

His height seemed to grow, if that was at all possible. 'And you have no business being mad at an eight-year-old for a mistake *you* made. Grow up.'

The words stung. How could he possibly understand the complete heart-stopping fear of looking in her rearview mirror and realising a child wasn't there? It was if she'd forgotten how to breathe until she turned the corner and saw his small figure on the doorstep. 'He frightened the life out of me!'

'Then giving out to him is hardly the best way of showing that, is it?'

After his dangerously calm statement, her mouth opened—but nothing came out. So she closed it again. Then she looked down at Johnnie's bent head and a wave of guilt washed over her. What was she doing?

She stepped forward, her tone softening. 'I really did think you'd got into the car, Johnnie.'

The boy raised his chin, blinked at her and then mumbled, 'Sorry.'

Teagan's throat went tight. It wasn't her nephew's fault that she'd been so harassed that morning. It wasn't his fault that it had taken for ever to get everyone dressed, or that his five-year-old sister had then spilt cereal all over herself. Which had led to yet another change of clothes. It wasn't his fault that his aunt really couldn't juggle her work with three children. No matter how much it killed her that she couldn't. She should have been so much better at this. Women all over the world did it, so why couldn't she? She'd never felt so inferior.

Hunkering down in front of him and looking him straight in the eye, she tried to explain. 'No, *I'm* sorry. I should have seen you weren't in the car. When I realised you weren't there I was scared silly.' She took a breath, her voice wobbling. 'I pretty much suck at being an aunt, don't I?'

Johnnie smiled a small smile. 'You're doin' all right.' Then he glanced up at Brendan. 'See ya.'

Just like that, he had forgotten all about it.

'See ya.' Brendan watched as he walked to the car, pulled open the door and hauled himself in, all the while aware that Teagan had stood up next to him and was glaring in his direction.

But the sight of her obvious guilt had backed him down. She was obviously finding this tough. He tried a smile, his eyes moving from her ruffled hair to the shadows she hadn't quite managed to disguise beneath her eyes. 'Rough morning?'

'None of your damn business.'

So much for trying to be nice. One large hand caught her arm as she turned to go back to the car. 'I did offer help.'

'I'm doing just fine.' She yanked her arm away.

'Obviously not, or you wouldn't have just abandoned a child.' If this was going to be his last trip across the street then he was damn well going to point out a few home truths while he was there. 'You're not used to kids. I get that. But you're so stubborn and determined to be Wonder Woman that when it comes to accepting help you're prepared to cut off your nose to spite your face. What have I ever done that makes my help such an awful proposition?'

Her face flamed while she searched for words.

Brendan shook his head, his voice dropping. 'All this because of one kiss a million years ago?'

It was the tone of his voice as much as the question. If she'd found him less of an all-round great guy to begin with she might have found it easier to tell him to go to hell after that long-ago kiss. Might have just fobbed him off with something about dating her flatmate's ex not being a good idea. It was what she should have done. But it had been easier to just let things slide, never encouraging him to talk to her again or allowing herself to be left alone in his company. Until their separate uni courses had ended and life had taken them in different directions.

It had been a lifetime ago. And yet, with him standing right in front of her, in the here and now, it felt as if it had been yesterday.

Thing was, her life seemed to be falling apart at the seams now. All of her precious control taken away from her by the presence of three small, demanding individuals.

And if she'd found the unwanted attraction she'd had for Brendan difficult to deal with when she had been young, and believed herself to *be* in control of the rest of her life, then it had to follow that now, when the rest of her life was falling apart, she would take some of her frustrations out on the only other person who had ever made her lose control. Even if that loss of control had only been for a few brief moments.

It was unfair of her, though, when all he'd done was steal one kiss, as he'd put it, *'a million years ago'*. The thought increased her frustration. And in turn she got even angrier with him.

How dared he go being all reasonable with her, in that deep, sensual voice of his?

'Why can't you just mind your own business like everyone else in this world?'

Damned if he knew. 'Why can't *you* just accept a simple offer of help when it's offered?'

'I've got to where I am now without any help from anyone. I'm not about to start looking for it now.'

A small frown creased Brendan's brow at the statement she'd accompanied with a stubborn set of her slight shoulders. He searched her eyes with his, and for the briefest of moments he saw a flash of pain there. Before she blinked long lashes and hid herself behind the carefully controlled mask she wore so well. And he wanted to know why. Why was she on her own? Why had there never been anyone there to help her before?

'Even the Lone Ranger had Tonto.'

She blinked in confusion. 'What?'

'No man is an island. Everyone needs a friend. How many of these clichés do you need me to quote at you before you admit they're true?' He took a breath, glanced past her to the three small figures in her car, and then back again into her emerald eyes. 'You're doing this to help out your sister because she needed help. I was just offering some of the same thing to an old friend.'

'What's in it for you?'

He ran a hand back through his hair in frustration, 'For crying out loud, Teagan. Can't I just be neighbourly?'

When she gaped at him he ploughed ahead. 'I don't know what it's been like for you over the years. But where I've been neighbours help each other, and they don't look for payment in return any further than the same consideration if they need help some time.'

Teagan continued to gape. Then snapped her mouth shut. She *did* need some help.

It wasn't just a case of wanting to prove she could do everything herself, was it? Because the simple fact was that if he'd been another neighbour, *any* other neighbour, she'd probably have accepted his help in a heartbeat.

The problem lay with her. And the fact that she hadn't been able to forget the effect that one simple kiss under the mistletoe had had on her. Even after all the years between.

She was the one still obsessing over an old attraction to him. *He* was just trying to be neighbourly.

Surely she'd grown up enough to have the maturity *not* to cut off her own nose to spite her face?

Taking a deep breath, she jumped into unknown territory. That place where people reached out for a helping hand. 'Okay.'

Brendan blinked at her for a brief second, suspicious of the turnaround. 'Okay?'

'Okay. I could use some help.'

His smile was slow. 'See, now, was that so difficult?'

He would never know. She exhaled. 'You start right now. I'm so late it's not even funny. But I warn you, if they keep you going the way they have me this morning, your chances of getting anything done 'til I get back are slim.'

'That's okay; I'm fairly up to date with work. I have time. That's the beauty of being the boss in a job you can do at home.'

Teagan knew he'd done well with the knowledge from his computer course in uni. Yet *another* success under his belt was his website design work. She forced a small, resentful smile at the fact that *he* was up to date in *his* work, 'I hate you for that.'

'Nah.' He smiled one of his more charming grins, winking at her as he walked past. 'You don't hate me. You like me. You always did. You just don't much like that fact right this minute, is all.'

Teagan wondered if he ever got tired of being right. But

as she turned to unload the children from her car she was already having to admit to herself that he was right about one very crucial fact.

She *did* like him. Always had. But she could like him from a distance and that would be fine with her. When her nephew and nieces went home, so could he.

She couldn't take a chance on ending up being friends with him again. Because look where that had got her last time…

CHAPTER FOUR

BAD idea. Oh, yeah. *Huge.*

She knew it the minute she walked back through her door that evening and found him asleep on her sofa.

He had no business looking that good on her sofa. Or in her house. Or anywhere else for that matter.

Slipping her heels off her aching feet by the door, she padded silently across the carpet and sat down on the armchair facing him. She allowed herself to study him at leisure. As if it was some kind of a rare and illicit treat, like chocolate to someone on a diet.

She started her study at the top. He had always had great hair. As blond as any golden boy's hair should be, and sun-kissed in places, which was rare in a country where it seemed to rain ninety-five per cent of the time. She remembered it when it had been longer and less tamed. And even now, as her eyes moved across it in its shorter style, she could still see the odd trace of a restless curl or two.

Her eyes moved down over his face. Asleep, he looked like he had at twenty-two, all boyish good looks with cheeks vaguely flushed in sleep. He'd had flushed cheeks a lot back in the day, from playing football on a winter's afternoon and jogging across the campus to make a class.

But she now knew that when he was awake he had laughter lines at the edges of his eyes, and deep grooves that appeared in his cheeks when he smiled. There was nothing boyish about that. It gave him depth, maturity. She decided she quite liked that.

Her gaze moved down to the sensual sweep of his mouth and swiftly past the memories attached to that part of him.

As for his body...

He *really* had no business looking so good. For the sake of decency the least he could have done was age badly. How did someone who spent that much time in front of a computer not put on a ton and a half of weight? *C'mon!*

With a small moan, he rolled towards her, and she held her breath, staying as silent as possible so she could look at him for longer. While it was safe.

But with a flicker of dark blond lashes his eyes opened, and he blinked slowly at her. When he spoke his voice was laced with sleep, deep and sensual. 'You're home.'

The two words struck a chord deep inside her, 'Yes, I'm home.'

He pushed himself onto one elbow and studied her with several slow blinks. 'You look less harassed than the last time I saw you.'

Teagan smiled, easing as she discussed a subject she still had some control over. 'The presentation went well. I think we got the contract.'

'That's good.'

Forcing her eyes to look away from the familiar dark blue ones that sparkled across at her, she quietly cleared her throat and asked, 'How were the terrors?'

Brendan smiled. 'Grand. Though I don't know who was more tired by the time they went to bed.'

'Oh, I know how that goes.'

He propped himself up on an elbow. 'How do you think people do this every day?'

'I really don't know.' She smiled again. 'Maybe you should ask your mother for us.'

'I thought girls picked up all this stuff from their own mothers?'

It was a fair enough assumption. And in the world he'd grown up in that was probably exactly how things worked. But Teagan hadn't grown up in that world.

All Teagan's mother had taught her was how to be old before her time, how to shoulder responsibilities that should never have been hers. But most of all she had taught her to be guarded, to measure everything she did and, most of all, never to make the same mistakes she had.

While she looked across at Brendan she wondered what he would think if he knew all that. It had been easier not to tell him when they'd been friends before. To allow him to believe that hers had been the same normal childhood that he and the rest of their group of friends had had.

University had been the first place she'd had where she could live in a world of partial make-believe.

'Maybe you should just get married and have kids of your own, and then you could tell me what it's like when the package is introduced gradually.'

His eyes flickered towards the floor, the thick lashes shadowing them for a second as he smiled wryly. 'Nah. I already tried the marriage thing. It didn't go so well.'

Teagan's eyes widened in surprise as he pushed up into a sitting position and swung his long legs over the edge of the sofa. 'I didn't know.'

'No, I don't suppose you would. We haven't exactly been pen-pals over the years.'

That they hadn't. But surely she would have heard

through the old grapevine? From the sporadic phone calls that had shared information on who was doing what. She had even had lunches with some of the old crowd from time to time. But then, why would anyone have thought to tell her? She'd made it abundantly clear she hadn't wanted anything more to do with one Brendan McNamara.

He shrugged his wide shoulders and looked back into her eyes. 'Don't worry about it. These things happen.'

Yes, they did. But to someone who had always succeeded at everything he did it must have been quite a blow. The part of her that had been his friend once, and the part of her that didn't like to see others in pain, immediately reached out to try and offer some words of comfort. 'It must have been tough on you, though. I am sorry. Really.'

There was another shrug as he reached for his shoes. 'No one ever wants a marriage to end.'

'I don't suppose they do.'

With an upward glance, he smiled wryly. 'Don't worry, I'm not about to add to your current woes by weeping all over your carpet. It was a while ago.'

'How long?' The question came out of her mouth before her brain kicked into gear and let her take the escape route he'd just offered her with his flat tone.

'A while.' He frowned at her briefly, then pushed himself to his feet and glanced around the room. 'You working again tomorrow?'

'Yes.' Unlike most of the rest of the nine to five world, she always worked a half-day on a Saturday. She'd never thought anything about it; it was just what she did. But then she'd never needed to make quality time for anyone. 'I'm done by lunchtime, though, so…?'

He nodded curtly as he located his sweater. 'No problem.'

Teagan watched as he pulled the sweater over his head,

her eyes taking in the movement of the muscles in his arms, the very brief glimpse of washboard waist as his T-shirt rose. And while she was watching she failed to notice when his head reappeared and he caught her watching.

Their eyes met and they stared at each other. Teagan could practically feel the static electricity.

Brendan blinked a couple of times, his gaze still steady. 'You never married, then?'

'No.' Her heart beat a little louder in her chest at the statement, even though he'd already asked her once before. She could almost hear the can of worms opening with a 'pop' in the background.

'How come?'

She shrugged her shoulders. 'Just not for me, I guess.'

'No one serious, then?'

'No.' And this conversation needed to stop soon. Nervously, she ran the tip of her tongue across her dry lips, glancing away. 'No one serious.'

His voice dropped. 'How come?'

It wasn't exactly the kind of intimate conversation she'd planned on having with him the next time she saw him. And she should really just tell him to mind his own damn business. Not that that had worked so far. But somehow the fact that he had told her about his failed marriage, even in passing, made him more human to her. Not that she was about to jump in with all her own deep psychological reasons for being single.

So she went with the first easy reason she could think of under pressure. 'Not everyone thinks that marriage is an immediate ticket to the land of fulfilment.'

His small snort of laughter brought her eyes back to his face in time for her to see the twist of his lips. 'Oh, I'm aware of that.'

She grimaced. 'Oh, Brendan, I'm sorry. I'm usually more sensitive to other people's feelings than that.'

He considered her words, and then answered them with a blunt, 'Are you?'

The question put her back up. Did she come across *that* cold and unthinking? She straightened her spine in the soft chair. 'Yes, as a matter of fact, I am.'

'Then how come you don't seem to realise that your nephew has the impression you don't like kids much?'

'What?'

Ignoring her widening eyes, Brendan moved back a step and sat back down on the edge of the sofa, facing her. 'I thought it was just the fact that he was ticked off at you for putting them to bed earlier than he's used to, but there were a few more comments made today. And he's for ever stopping the other two from playing, insisting they have to be quiet and not make a mess or Auntie Teagan will get mad.'

Teagan stared at him in shock. 'He does that?'

Brendan nodded. 'I think he thinks that if they're not on their best behaviour then you'll try to shunt them off somewhere else. They're bound to be feeling insecure enough as it is, what with their own mother disappearing and all.'

'She hasn't *disappeared*!' Teagan jumped to her sister's defence, as she had done for most of their lives. 'She's trying to save her marriage, for crying out loud!'

'And hasn't rung her own kids for three days. How do you think that makes them feel?'

All right, so that part was bugging her too. But had she been so busy just trying to get through the basic stuff each day that she hadn't thought to take care of the emotional welfare of the three small beings entrusted to her? The question she asked herself shocked her to the core. She, the one person who should know when someone needed to be reassured like that. If it had been Eimear in her care, as in days of old, she would have been there every night to comfort her, to reassure her, to hold her in her arms and tell her that she was loved.

Had she become so insular in her own independence that she now couldn't even cater to the most basic emotional needs of someone else in her care? *Damn it!*

Without thinking about the fact that Brendan was still in front of her, she allowed the tears to well at the back of her eyes. She was failing them. Not only could she not manage to make her own lifestyle accommodate her nieces and nephew when they needed her, she was also doing something she had never in her whole life thought she would do. She was failing in a promise made to her sister.

Brendan frowned when the first tear spilled over her lashes. He leaned closer to her, resting his elbows on his knees. 'Hey. C'mon, Teagan, don't do that. I just thought you should know.'

Teagan sniffed and turned her head to one side as she brushed the errant tear from her cheek. 'You're right. I should know. But, more to the point, I should have thought about it myself before now.'

'You were frazzled; you're not used to this. That's all.' He kept his voice low while forcing himself not to move closer to her and offer her a hug of comfort. Despite the strong urge he had to do just that. Somehow he knew she wouldn't be comfortable with that any more than the fiercely independent twenty-one-year-old from years ago would have been. 'Sometimes it takes an outsider to see things clearly.'

She shook her head. 'They were entrusted to my care. It's my job to see these things.'

'You're only human, honey. We all make mistakes.'

Ignoring the small endearment, she glanced in his direction. 'You don't understand.'

'Try me.'

She shook her head again, forced the tears down from her eyes into her throat and swallowed them away. 'I should have thought about it more, instead of worrying about the effect their being here was having on my own life. It was selfish of me.'

'No.' He said the word slowly. 'It was selfish of your sister to dump them on you without more warning. If you'd had more time to plan you could have taken some time off work and spent quality time with them. That would have stopped this from ever happening.'

Again she immediately felt the need to defend Eimear. 'She wouldn't have asked me if it wasn't an emergency.'

'And if I had to guess I'd say that you've probably spent most of your life bailing her out in an emergency—haven't you?' A fair eyebrow quirked in question.

How could he know that?

He smiled. 'You don't have to answer. I can see it on your face.'

Teagan swallowed again, and opened her mouth to say something more in her sister's defence. But Brendan took a breath and spoke. This time in a silkily persuasive tone. 'I have an idea, though. That could help fix this some.'

Her eyes narrowed with suspicion. 'What kind of an idea?'

CHAPTER FIVE

'YOU'RE having fun. Admit it.'

Teagan smiled and hoisted Meghan up against her waist. 'Okay, I'm having fun.' She glanced at Brendan from the corner of her eye. 'But, more importantly, *they're* having fun. That's what this is all about, after all.'

She watched as Johnnie took Katie's hand and dragged her across to look at the monkey enclosure. For the first time in her life Teagan had called in sick to her workplace when she wasn't really sick. But it was worth the feeling of guilt she'd had when she made the call to see the joy on the children's faces when they had arrived at Dublin Zoo. And to hear the laughter that had ensued ever since.

The trip had been a stroke of genius. And she had Brendan to thank for it.

'Thank you. This was a great idea.' Which would probably not have been half as much fun if he hadn't been there. He'd made it fun all day.

He stopped in his tracks and turned to look at her with a smile on his face. 'You're very welcome.'

The smile was infectious, and Teagan couldn't help but laugh. 'You're really not for real, are you?'

Raising his large hands, he patted his palms along the front of his chest. 'I'm very definitely real.'

She shook her head. 'You're having as much fun with this as they are. A grown man having fun at the zoo. That's why you're so good with them; mentally you're the same age.'

He laughed. 'Ah, no, you can't go blaming that old "men are kids at heart" thing. It's the *zoo*, Teagan. It's compulsory to have fun here. You can't tell me you grew up in Dublin and didn't come here before.'

'I did.' She looked across at the children again, to make sure they were still safely within her sight. 'The school had a trip here once.'

His eyes followed the same path as hers. 'We came here every time we came to Dublin with my parents. It was a sort of annual family trip.'

With her eyes still on the children, she began to walk forwards as they moved to the next enclosure. 'That must have been nice for you.'

There was something in her tone as she said the words that sparked his attention. Something underlying— perhaps even a small current of resentment? What was with that?

Curious, he fell into step beside her, adjusting his usual long stride to hers. 'You're quite the mystery, Teagan Delaney.'

'Am I?'

'Oh, yeah.'

'Just because I didn't make an annual visit to the zoo?'

He smiled. 'Well, there's that. Then there's the fact that you honestly didn't believe that you would enjoy this, did you?'

'I will admit to having my doubts when you talked me into it.'

'And it nearly killed you to pull a sickie, didn't it?'

Another turn of her head in his direction. 'Oh, yes.'

'Mmm.' He nodded his head, gave her a quick glance as he pursed his lips in thought, then asked, 'So the mystery would be how someone your age has managed to get this far in life without taking the odd sick day to have some fun?'

'I have fun,' she answered, with an almost petulant pout of her bottom lip. 'I have loads of fun.'

Brendan quirked a brow in disbelief. 'Doing what?'

'My work is fun. I get to travel to all sorts of great places, all over the world, and meet loads of interesting people. That's fun.'

'That's travel agent fun.'

'Corporate travel consultant fun, if you don't mind. It's still fun, though.'

'It's not the same as taking a day to go play with kids at the zoo, though.'

'No, I don't suppose it is.' And she knew he was right about that. Did he *ever* get tired of being right? Though with the new information she'd gleaned the night before she also had to wonder if being right about so many other things was any consolation for having been so wrong about one very big thing.

Even so, he was on the money with the zoo trip. And about how little time she had ever taken with her nephew and nieces to have this kind of fun before. Not that she hadn't spent time with them. She always made time at Christmas, and on their birthdays. She was very conscientious about those kinds of things. But it wasn't quite the same, was it?

Which made her wonder if it was something lacking in her personality that stopped her from having this kind of fun, or if she had merely kept herself at arm's length from them to avoid any more responsibility for others in her life? Had she been trying to distance herself from an emotional attachment to them? Lord, was she so very defensive now that three little kids were seen as a threat in some way?

How sad did that make her?

'Oh, no, you don't.' Brendan's voice sounded close beside her as he stopped and took Meghan from her arms, to bounce her a couple of times before holding her close. 'No going all introverted today.'

'I wasn't.' She watched with a small smile as Meghan laughed and cooed up at him. Apparently his attractiveness to women started very young.

'Yeah, you were. I remember that look. You used to do that when I knew you before—fade off into Teagan world.'

A flush crept up over her cheeks. 'I can't help it if I'm a highly intelligent woman who does a lot of thinking.'

'I'm not saying you're not intelligent. I'm just saying you have a tendency to think too much.' He nuzzled Meghan's dark curls and spoke in a baby voice. 'Yes, she does—doesn't she, Meggie?'

'And *you* don't think about things?'

'I think plenty. But I try not to obsess.'

'You think I do?'

'Yes, I do.' Meghan was jiggled up and down again in time to his, 'Yes-I-do-indeed.'

They stopped in unison, a few steps away from where the older children had discovered a play area. After a moment, Teagan sighed. 'Okay. Maybe I do.'

Brendan smiled softly at the confession. 'See, now we're making some headway, don't you think?'

Her focus still on the children, Teagan scowled a little. 'You see this day as some kind of therapy session for me, do you?'

'Maybe for all of us. The kids needed a day of fun with

you, *Auntie* Teagan. And their Auntie Teagan certainly needed a day of fun with them. And I needed an excuse to get to the zoo again. My mother stopped taking us when the youngest hit eighteen or nineteen. It was a traumatic time for me.'

'Poor you.'

After a moment of silence Brendan turned sideways and studied her profile. 'Can I ask you a question?'

'*Now* you're asking permission?' She looked at him with a teasing light to her eyes.

He smiled right back. 'I think I've been fairly lucky to get away with so much so far, haven't I?'

'Yes, you have.'

'Well, then, maybe it's better if I ask for permission before I ask you something big.'

Her mouth went dry. *Uh-oh.* What was he going to ask?

She had to clear her throat before she spoke. 'On what subject?'

'Ah, now, in telling you that I'd be asking the question, and I haven't actually been given permission yet, have I?'

Wise guy. She took a breath and let her curiosity get the better of her. 'Go on, then.'

'What happened with us?'

She gaped at him. *Well, hell.*

'We were pretty good friends, I thought.'

She found her voice. 'Yes, we were.'

'So what happened?'

Turning her face away, she blinked as she mulled over the least dangerous of answers she could give him. After all, between the help he'd given her of late and the *entente cordiale* they seemed to have going in the here and now, she was loath to ruin it all by knocking him back with something blunt. Like the *Just leave it alone* that was on the tip of her tongue.

'People just drift apart sometimes.'

Brendan knew a cop-out when he heard one. 'And that's what you're saying happened with us?'

She glanced back at him.

He shook his head. 'I'm not buying that.'

'It doesn't really matter now.'

'I think it does, or you wouldn't have been trying so hard to keep me at arm's length since I moved in across the road from you.'

His statement hit a nerve. He could see it from the slight rise of her delicate chin. What he'd said earlier about her being a mystery was true. Something had changed the night before, when he'd confronted her about the way she was with the children. He'd touched on something big and he just knew it. And the part of him that had found it so difficult to just stay away from her was all the more intrigued by what that something was. Had he really known her at all when he'd thought he had before?

Which had brought him back to a question that had haunted him for a very long time. So he'd finally allowed himself to ask it.

'Brendan—'

'Was kissing you such a bad thing?'

'Brendan—'

'No, come on. I'd like to know.' He braved a step closer to her, jiggling Meghan as he went. 'I wouldn't have done it if I hadn't thought—'

'Thought what?' Her tone was sharper, a defensive reaction to his persistence. 'That I was some kind of a sure thing? Did you think because we'd talked and formed some kind of tentative bond that it immediately meant I was primed, or something? The groundwork has been put in so she *must* be ready to fall at my feet—right?'

The jiggling stopped as he frowned at her reasoning. 'Teagan, it was one wee kiss under some mistletoe. It was hardly some big seduction scene. If I'd meant it to be that I'd have done one hell of a better job of it.'

It was the kind of arrogant statement that she'd never heard from him before. Which just annoyed her all the more. 'I'll just bet you weren't used to a girl who didn't fall at your feet. That must have made me fascinating to you.'

Bullseye. 'I wish I'd never asked now. That's not why I wanted to know.'

'Isn't it? You had dozens of girls chasing after you when you split up with Shannon. And yet you chose the one that wasn't chasing. What made you think that kissing me was such a great idea?'

Meghan whimpered, forcing Brendan to focus on her and recommence the jiggling she liked so much. He took a few long breaths and waited for their angry words to dissipate in the air between them. Then, with more calmness than he felt inside, he answered with a matter-of-fact tone. 'Because I'd been thinking about kissing you for a very long time. That just happened to be the first opportunity.'

Her green eyes widened in surprise.

Brendan smiled slowly. She hadn't expected that one, obviously. 'You didn't know that?'

Her head shook from side to side, the ends of her hair catching against her mouth.

He watched as she raised a hand to move the hair, his eyes focusing on her lips as she did it. And damn if he didn't feel a sudden urge to kiss her again. As if their heated conversation about it had suddenly made it a physical need.

This time he had the good sense not to try it. 'I wasn't looking for some quick fling with you. I cared about you back then—wanted something more than us being just good friends.'

'That's why it could never have worked.'

She seemed as surprised as him that she'd said what she had. With a few blinks of her dark lashes she turned her face from his and took a long, deep breath.

Brendan didn't understand. 'I don't understand.'

'I know you don't.' She forced her voice to stay strong. 'But that's the way it is. So there's no point talking about it.'

He still didn't understand. 'I still don't get it.'

She sighed, her chin dropping as she looked down at the ground with a small frown. 'I was never going to get involved with you. Not that way. So there was no point. It was better that I just stayed away from you, so you could move on and find someone else to fall for and live happily ever after.'

There was a brief moment of silence before he spoke. 'That didn't go so well.'

When she raised her head he had already turned away from her, and she felt a sudden need to reach out towards him, to say she was sorry that he hadn't got what he'd wanted. But it wasn't her fault. She had to stop trying to ease things for other people all the time. If she'd been a different person maybe it would have worked for them. Maybe being friends could have taken their relationship on into something deeper and more magical.

But Teagan didn't believe in magic. So what would have been the point?

'I wish it had worked out for you, Brendan, I really do.' Her voice was soft, almost a whisper as she voiced the heartfelt words. 'I know how much you wanted a family of your own one day. But that would never have happened with me, trust me. I don't know anything about what a happy family is like.'

She stared at the picture he presented, with the cherublike child in his arms, felt an ache in her chest she didn't want to feel. And then walked away to join the other children.

Brendan stood stock still as she left. He jiggled Meghan a few more times and avoided the chubby fingers that grabbed at his nose. As he watched Teagan join the children, saw how they immediately lit up in her presence, he felt a cramp in his chest so strong it almost made him catch his breath. She'd needed a shove in the right direction with this day-trip, but already she was opening up with them and they were flourishing under the strength of that attention.

If she really knew nothing about a happy family then her reaction to involvement certainly made more sense. She didn't trust herself to care, did she?

What he had to do now was decide whether or not he was prepared to try and give her a shove in the right direction one more time.

Because, heaven help him, all being with her did was make him want more. Again.

CHAPTER SIX

SHE was really starting to worry.

Eimear still hadn't called to see how the children were. And although Teagan could understand why that might have happened for the first few days, while she tried to sort out her problems with Mac, she doubted that her sister would have gone so long without a single phone call.

And the underlying current of tension in the air with Brendan wasn't helping her.

While worrying about her sister was a constant niggle in her mind, being in Brendan's company since their conversation at the zoo was an unwanted constant and burning ache.

She was walking a thin line between control and screaming like a Banshee. And it was now beginning to tell on her work.

'Are you all right, Teagan?'

She glanced up from her computer screen at Stephen Connolly, her boss of eight years. 'I'm fine—why?'

He perched himself on the edge of her desk and quirked an eyebrow at her. 'You just don't seem yourself at the minute. And I heard you were sick on Saturday...'

She felt a pang of guilt to add to all the emotions currently churning around inside her body. For a brief second all the churning *did* make her feel sick. 'I'm fine.'

'If you've caught a bug or some such thing then you should take some time off. It's not like you take sick days at short notice.'

Her eyes avoided his and focused instead on the booking information on her screen. She scrolled down through the employee names from the corporation they had booked a conference in Spain for. It was in a super hotel, where she herself had stayed twice—one of the perks of the job. That, and the varying places all over the world it had taken her to, had kept her from having too much time on her hands to think lonely thoughts. Until recently. 'I'm just trying to make sure I have this perfect before I send it in. It's a big booking.'

Stephen glanced at the screen, leaning forward a couple of inches to add to the intimacy of his lowered tone. 'Teagan?'

She raised her eyes. 'Yes?'

'I don't ever have to worry about how good you are at your job. You're the best here.'

She flushed at the praise.

'But the thing about a good boss is that I have to watch out for my best employees, and right now I'm worried that you're pushing yourself too hard.' He studied her face. 'What can I do to help?'

Teagan swallowed, and forced herself not to cry in front of yet another man. What was with her of late? It wasn't as if she could even blame it on PMT.

One of the reasons she'd stayed so long with her current employer was the fact that she'd always felt part of a team, not like just an employee. They all worked together to make their targets, burned the midnight oil together when it was called for and partied when things were going well. It was a family of sorts.

The grey-haired man currently perched on her desk was the patriarch of that family. The closest thing she'd had to a genuinely caring father figure.

'You need to take some time off?'

The very thought of doing that would normally have scared the life clean out of her. Her work was the most important thing in her life. Or at least had been. But, having spent time with the children over the weekend, she felt a tug towards them now that she was back in the office. It had been bad on Monday, but now, by Wednesday, it was awful. Almost as if they were her own children and she was being forced away from them. How on earth, she wondered, did the mother of a newborn do it?

It was something she'd never allowed herself to wonder about before.

'I think maybe I do. I'm sorry, Stephen.'

'Nonsense.' He patted her hand where it sat on the computer's mouse. 'It's about time you took some time for yourself. We all need it from time to time, and I've always said you work entirely too hard.'

Teagan smiled affectionately at him. 'Thanks. I'll take this stuff home with me and e-mail it in.'

'That's fine.' He stood up, turning to walk back to his own office. Then he stopped and looked back at her. 'Take as long as you need. You know your job is always here.'

She was suddenly very grateful for her substitute family. But the simple fact was that she had a family of sorts who right that minute was more important.

'You're home early.'

She smiled at the scene that greeted her, where a week ago she'd have been horrified. Her normally neat and ordered living room was scattered with cushions and blankets, with children's faces peeking out all over the place. It looked as if she'd been burgled.

'Hi, Auntie Teagan! Come play with us.'

Dropping her bag on the floor, and setting her folder of work on the table, she smiled down at Katie. 'What are you playing?'

Johnnie crawled out from under a blanket. 'We made tents in the jungle.'

Katie giggled. 'Brendan is a monster.'

Teagan grinned, her dimples flashing. 'Oh, I *know*.'

He smiled a very adult smile at her.

Which she met with a very childish poking out of her tongue. An action so out of character she even giggled when she'd done it.

He laughed. 'Come on, then—come play.'

Somehow the invitation took on a whole new meaning when he said it. Her mind formed a very vivid mental image of the kind of games two consenting adults could play surrounded by soft cushions and blankets.

Brendan saw the flush that touched her cheeks and continued to smile. 'Don't be shy.'

'Pleeeeaaassse, Auntie Teagan.' Katie jumped up and down and held her hands together to add to the pleading, which sent out a wave of throaty giggles from Meghan, where she was crawling about on the floor.

Teagan honestly couldn't remember the last time she had done something so completely childish. It felt awkward to her even thinking about it. Where did she begin?

'Chicken.'

His challenge forced her forward. Slipping her heels off her feet, she didn't even stop to think of the consequences that crawling around on the floor would have on her linen trousers. With a scowling face and pursed lips combination she intended to look scary, she crawled after Katie, who in turn squealed loudly and crawled off into a 'tent'.

Twenty minutes later she was exhausted and completely dishevelled. And she'd had a blast.

The older children were yelling something about juice, while Meghan snored loudly from the sofa, and as Brendan appeared under the blanket 'tent' with her he shouted, 'Think of the OAPs and bring some for us too, please.'

'They'll murder the kitchen now, you know.' Leaning back against the sofa-edge, Teagan gripped the front of her shirt and flapped it back and forth in an attempt to cool down.

'There's a pretty good chance.' He settled down beside her, shoulder to shoulder, and with a grin he poked her in the ribs, 'You certainly helped with the mess in here, though, miss.'

'I did, didn't I?' She giggled and squirmed away from his touch.

Brendan quirked an eyebrow, an outrageous twinkle of mischief in his eyes. 'Are you ticklish, perchance?'

'*No.*'

She'd answered too quickly, and his teeth glinted in the soft light of the 'tent'. 'Yes.' He reached for her ribs again. 'You.' And on her other side as she squirmed and laughed. 'Are.'

'Stop.' She laughed and tried to squirm free. 'Seriously!'

When she tried to roll away from him he pinned her with one long arm and continued his torture with the other hand, until tears were rolling down her face and her throat was sore from laughing.

Then he stopped.

He was over her, his upper body holding her beneath him, her breasts crushed against him. And they were both breathing hard. And staring.

They'd managed to forget the tension between them for the briefest of time. But suddenly Teagan felt it was back.

The smile fading from his face, Brendan continued to look into her eyes as he moved his hand from the ticklish spot at the base of her ribcage. He smoothed his palm along the side of her body, curving in at her waist and then sweeping out until his hand rested against her hip.

Oh, yeah. The tension was back, all right.

The muscles in her stomach tingled. He was thinking about kissing her, wasn't he? The thing was, unlike the moment years ago when she'd had the same realisation, this time there was no voice in the back of her mind saying, 'Oh, no.' She *wanted* to be kissed.

Just that simple. Nothing more. Just kissed. By Brendan. In a makeshift tent on her living room floor.

One afternoon of messing about with three kids and Brendan in a *faux* family scene and the part of her that was so commitment phobic seemed to have taken a momentary hike.

She knew there would be consequences to a kiss when she still didn't want a relationship with him. But it didn't stop her from wanting the kiss. From wanting to find a way to break the tension.

Damn, but he wanted to kiss her. He really did. But she'd run a mile, wouldn't she?

His gaze dropped to her lips, watched with fascination as the end of her tongue appeared and damped them with one smooth stroke. And her doing *that* wasn't helping his self-control any.

He smoothed his thumb unconsciously against her hip, felt the rise and fall of her breasts against him as she breathed. Hell. He knew sexual tension when he felt it. Should know rightly what to do about it at his age.

And she wasn't exactly running away this time, was she? *Maybe—*

'We brung you juice.'

Brendan closed his eyes for a brief second. It was a case of the cavalry arriving, he guessed. He opened his eyes and found Teagan smiling up at him.

'Saved by the juice,' she whispered.

'Thanks, Katie. We'll be right out.'

'We'll put it on the table.'

Brendan smiled back at Teagan. 'Thanks, Johnnie.'

But even though there was the clink of glasses being left on the tabletop they didn't move.

After a moment, Brendan aimed them in the general direction of normal conversation. 'How do you think parents manage to get time to fool around?'

Teagan glanced towards the gap in their tent and then looked back at him. 'I really don't know.'

Taking a moment to rearrange his large body by her side, he continued to move his thumb back and forth against her hip as he asked in a low, deep rumble, 'What were your parents like?'

She stiffened.

He continued to move his thumb back and forth in soothing strokes. 'That bad?'

Teagan nodded with a single quirk of her eyebrows.

'Tell me about it?'

She shook her head. 'I'd really rather not.'

'Are they still around?'

'No.' She took a breath and looked up at the blanket above her head, reciting the facts like a shopping list. 'My mother died when I was sixteen. My father, six years ago.'

'I'm sorry.' He said the words looking into her eyes, his gaze sure and steady. 'That must have been rough.'

'It was rougher when they were alive and together, if you want me to be perfectly honest about it.'

The deadpan tone to her voice didn't escape him as he started to put some pieces together. 'Is that why you decided you'd never get into a serious relationship?'

It was yet another of those probing, too close to home questions that he was so good at asking of late. She should have used it as an invitation to move away from him and shut him out again. But somehow, with the gentle touch of his hand against her hip and the safe cocoon of the blanket around them, she didn't feel the urge to run.

Maybe if she told him a little he would understand her reasoning better and realise that he wouldn't change her mind? Even though two minutes before she'd been more than ready to be kissed by him.

She took a breath. It was worth a try. 'Yes.'

'You wouldn't make the same mistakes as them, though.'

'No, I definitely wouldn't. But it's easier to be on my own.'

Brendan was almost disappointed in her reasoning. Where was her fight? When he'd known her before she'd been feisty and determined in everything she aimed herself at. And that drive had certainly served her well in her career, 'Have you ever actually tried?'

'I've had relationships.' The thought that he saw her as some sad and lonesome spinster irked her. She *had* dated, after all. She'd just not dated anyone who might look for anything serious, that was all.

'But you made damn sure they weren't long-lasting, right?'

Oh, good. Now he could read her mind. She didn't reply to the question.

'You might be missing out on something great, though. Don't you think?'

'That "someone for everyone" theory?'

His head nodded.

Turning her head into a more comfortable position, she narrowed her eyes and asked, 'And you still believe that after a broken marriage?'

It was a fair enough question. He kept looking her straight in the eye as he answered. 'I have to believe it. I just got it wrong the first time round, is all. People make mistakes. It doesn't mean that there's not still magic out there somewhere.'

She blinked. 'You've been spending way too much time with the children reading fairy stories.'

'And you are such a cynic it's almost sad.'

'No, I'm a realist. It's the world we live in that's sad.'

He felt his heart twist as the shutters came back down over her eyes. She was closing him out again, and he didn't want to be closed out. All those very brief openings did was leave him wanting more. Leave him wanting to prove she was wrong. Maybe for himself as much as for her. Which was a leap, considering that up until a year ago he'd probably have agreed with a lot of the things she was saying now.

She tried to move away from him, so he tightened his hold on her hip. 'Do you still think that with those three great kids out there? You had fun with them today. You laughed as much as they did. Nothing sad there.'

'They're great kids.'

'They're amazing kids. And there's a certain amount of magic in that, isn't there?'

He was right.

'A lot of that is thanks to Eimear. She adores them.'

'But not enough to ring and see how they are.' A small frown creased between his eyes as he looked beyond his annoyance at her sister's behaviour to the new information he now had. 'She has stuff to deal with from your growing up too, doesn't she?'

It was the first understanding he'd shown of her sister, and that softened Teagan against his side. She glanced towards the gap in the blanket and raised her head an inch to listen for the children. Just about catching the sound of their voices in the kitchen, she set her head back down and decided to confide in Brendan one more time. It was getting to be a habit.

'Yes, she does. But she wouldn't go this long without calling them.' The niggle in her stomach returned. 'I'm worried.'

'You think there's something wrong?'

The niggle became a bad dose of indigestion. 'I don't know. But it's not like her.'

'What can we do?'

We. It stunned her, the strength there was in such a small word. She'd never been a 'we' or an 'us'. It intimated at not being alone, at having someone to lean on in moments when she was scared or couldn't quite find the strength to get through. It suggested sharing and caring. At intimacy on a level that went way beyond the physical.

And it scared her.

Her voice went cool. 'I've taken some time off work so I can sort things out.'

'Well, then, we'll see if we can find her.'

There he went with the 'we' thing again.

'No, it's okay. You've given up enough of your time as it is. I can take it from here.'

It was like a slap in the face. He slowly removed his hand from her hip. 'I see.'

Teagan felt her heart twist painfully at the tone to his voice, so she backtracked some. 'It's not that I don't appreciate what you've done...'

He nodded and pushed his body away from her. 'Right.'

She closed her eyes when he began to unfold his large frame and remove himself from the cocoon they'd been sharing. Somehow she had to find a way of letting him know how much his help had meant to her, while not encouraging him too much. Because there had always been a time when she was going to let him go again, hadn't there?

But somehow the letting him go wasn't as easy as she'd planned. Even the thought of it was already an ache on top of an older ache.

Inside a few brief moments she'd scrambled out and stood up, smoothing her hands along her trousers. He was already tying his trainers on, sitting in the one chair left free.

'I'm sure the children would like it if you stayed for dinner.'

He didn't look up. 'The children. Right.'

His coldness, and the ache in her chest, forced frustration into her voice. 'What do you want from me, Brendan? I've already told you the way things are with me.'

'Yes, you have.' He finished tying his laces with an angry tug and then stood up suddenly, towering over her smaller frame. 'But what you haven't done is admit why you're so desperate to push me away every chance you get.'

She felt very small, overwhelmed by the sheer size and absolute maleness of him. With a fortifying breath, she tilted her head back to look up into his angry face. 'I've told you I don't want a serious relationship.'

'I haven't asked for a serious relationship in the here and now yet, have I?'

It was true, he hadn't. He'd said that that was what he

would have wanted in the past. But in the here and now all he'd done was try to be a friend, to get her to open up and trust him. He'd offered help and friendship. It was where that friendship would lead that worried her.

He took a step closer until his body almost touched hers. 'Face facts. You're pushing me away because you see me as a threat. Which means you must be attracted to me in some way.'

She held her ground, stayed perfectly still while her heart beat so hard she was sure he must be able to hear it. 'I wish we could be friends again. I do. But the last time we tried being friends you made a pass at me. Can you guarantee that won't happen again?'

The smile on his face didn't make it all the way to his eyes. 'If I'd made a pass at you five minutes ago under that dumb tent you'd have let me.'

When she said nothing he knew he'd hit his mark. He raised his head and glanced over her shoulder towards the kitchen, before dropping his voice and looking back at her face. 'And if it weren't for those children in there I'd prove that right this minute.'

Teagan stepped back. 'I think you should leave now.'

There was a flicker in his dark blue eyes. 'You think this is easy for me either, Teagan? The last thing I expected when I moved here was to see you again. And I'm no more ready for some deep involvement that might not work out than you are.'

'Then you can see there's no point in this going any further.'

'You see, that's where we differ.'

She frowned in confusion.

'Because I'm brave enough to try.'

'I don't want to try!' She snapped the words up at him.

'No, you're too scared to fail with someone. Because if you do, then what is there left worth fighting for? If you got lucky there might just be something pretty damned amazing here.'

'And there might just as well not be. Which would only prove me right.'

'But it's the amazing thing that's the scarier, isn't it? Because if you had that…' his voice softened as he reached a large hand to her face, ran a long finger along her jaw-line, from just below her ear to her chin, then moved away, '…you'd have to let go, wouldn't you, Teagan? And that's what's *really* scary.'

CHAPTER SEVEN

'TEAGAN, it's Mac. We've had an accident in the car.'

The world fell away from under her feet. No matter what reassurances Mac gave her about them both being 'all right now', it wasn't enough. She needed to be there and see for herself.

She hung up the phone in a daze. Then paced up and down for what felt like an age. Then, despite the air that had been between them when he'd last left her house, it was Brendan she went to without a single thought.

The face that greeted him at his front door knocked back the cool response he'd prepared when he saw her cross the street.

'What the hell—?'

'I need your help.' She was shaking as he reached out and tugged her through the doorway. 'I'm sorry.'

'Don't apologise.' He leaned his head down to examine her face with concerned eyes. 'What's happened? Is it one of the children?'

'No, they're fine. They're playing with Anne's kids, two doors down.'

'Then what is it?'

'It's Eimear. She was in an accident.'

Brendan's eyes widened. 'Is she okay?'

Teagan gulped and looked over his shoulder at the cof-
fee-coloured wall behind him. Somehow in her present
emotional state she doubted she could look him in the eye
as well. Not while he was using that soft tone and had his
hand on her arm, smoothing up and down in silent reassurance. It would just be too much. And she didn't deserve
it after the way things had been left between them.

She managed a nod. 'She's in hospital in Killarney.' With
a couple of blinks she dropped her chin and looked for one
of the nice, safe buttons on his shirt. 'I have to go see her.'

'Of course you do.'

'I know I have no right to ask, but I was wondering if
you could mind the children while I drive there?'

He was silent until she looked up into his eyes. 'I don't
think that's the best plan.'

How could he? He was going to use *this* as a way of
getting back at her? Teagan went cold.

'You're in no fit state to drive all that distance on your
own. I'll take you.'

It really was about time she had a little more faith in his
strength of character, wasn't it? Her heart thawed around
the edges at his concern. Was this what it would be like to
have someone like him around? Someone who thought
about her welfare, her needs?

But she had to think of three people more needy than
herself. 'I don't think the kids should come along just yet.
It might be too scary for them.'

'Have you told them?'

She shook her head. 'No. I only got the call a few
minutes ago. This was the first place I thought to come.'

The smile was immediate. His hand stopped its smoothing on her arm and squeezed once before departing. 'Let's

talk to Anne about them staying there for a couple of nights. She and James seem to be a great couple, from what I've seen, and the kids could see it as a sleepover. We'll be back before they know there's anything wrong.'

Already he was taking control, organising what needed to be done. And Teagan felt herself calm down. He was right. She was in no fit state to drive to Killarney. It was hours away and already hitting late afternoon as it was. It would be dark by the time she got there. The sensible, rational part of her mind realised there was a very good chance she'd panic the whole way there, and that didn't make for a safe driver.

But still there was another part of her that recognised that leaving them would make her the second important female figure to leave the children alone in a short space of time. And that didn't sit well on her. 'I don't think I can leave them with people they hardly know.'

'They've played with Anne's kids a lot these last few days. They'll be fine. Kids that age love sleepovers.'

How did he know they'd been going over there to play? Had he been spying on her?

He saw the thought cross her eyes and nodded just the once. 'Someone had to make sure you didn't leave one behind again.'

She opened her mouth to speak.

But he beat her to it. 'I'm going over to speak to Anne. You go pack a bag, and I'll come get you in a half-hour. The sooner we go, the sooner we'll be back.'

It took more than half an hour in the end. Teagan took a lot of time fussing, making sure the children had everything they might need. Come rain, snow, sleet or passing force ten gale. While the children barely dragged themselves away from their game to say goodbye.

It was only Meghan who clung to her with pudgy arms that held her neck in a vice grip.

Teagan smelled the fresh, baby talcum scent of her and held on, rocking her in her arms as tears welled in the back of her eyes.

'I'll be back really soon, Meggie, I promise.'

She felt a firm, warm hand against her back and then Brendan's deep voice sounded in her ear. 'We have to go, honey. Let me have her a minute.'

Meghan's arms loosened as Brendan looked down into her face. 'C'mon, angel, let's go bounce. You wanna bounce?'

Sweeping the beginnings of tears from her lashes, Teagan watched him bounce Meaghan up and down in a more exaggerated way than he had on their day at the zoo. He bounced some more until Anne's husband lifted her from his arms and repeated the bouncing, so Meghan barely had time to register the change-over. It was very clever, so very thoughtful. And it brought a lump to her throat.

As he turned towards her she smiled without any deeper thought than the fact that that was what he made her do. Simply by the things he did. He made her smile most when she saw him with the kids, especially Meghan. He would make one hell of a dad some day.

He was in front of her in two strides, his hand reaching out to cup her elbow. 'Let's get going.'

She nodded at his soft words and turned to Anne. 'I can't thank you en—'

'Then don't. Just go make sure your sister is okay. The kids will be grand here.'

Brendan was still mulling over the look she'd worn on

her face as Anne hugged her even as they left Dublin far behind. He glanced over at her where she sat, straight spine, in the seat beside him. 'Anne is very fond of you.'

'She's been a great neighbour and very friendly since I moved in.' And she had been even more so since she'd come back from a holiday with her husband and kids. If they'd been there earlier Teagan doubted she'd even have had to ask for help from Brendan at all. Timing was everything, she guessed...

'Not too close, though?'

No, not so close that they'd hugged before. The thoughtful gesture had caught her off guard. 'I don't have that many close friends outside of work these days.'

Was she so afraid of letting anyone into her life? Brendan looked out through the windscreen again as rain began to splatter it with tiny droplets. 'So I'm not the only one you keep at arm's length, then?'

There was a brief pause. 'No, I guess not.'

Concentrating on driving gave him time to take some small comfort from that fact. Then he asked with a softer voice, 'Tell me about Eimear?'

Even having her name spoken out loud seemed to make Teagan attempt to sit taller in her seat. 'What do you want to know?'

His peripheral vision caught the movement. 'Anything you think you can tell me without it starting another argument would be good. This could be a pretty long journey if we spend all of it not talking.'

She nodded, then a small smile touched her face and she softened her stance. 'She's beautiful. But then I'm a little biased, seeing as I was kind of a mother to her most of her life.'

'She's younger than you. I remember that much.' He

flicked on the windscreen wipers, glanced over long enough to see a nod in answer, and asked, 'By how much?'

'Four years. She was my parents' second attempt at making things better.'

Doing his maths, he realised that that would have made her twelve when their mother died. That had to have been tough—on both of them. 'She must have been quite young when she got married.'

It had been the source of their first real arguments. Teagan felt her eyes well up again as she remembered them now, while her sister lay in a hospital bed. 'They met when she was seventeen; they married when she was eighteen.'

Even younger than Teagan had been when she had first wrestled with her feelings for Brendan. But while Teagan had run away from Brendan, Eimear had run straight into the arms of the man *she* had cared for. And had ended up pregnant, then married, before she had taken the time to really know him. It had been the same mistake as their parents all over again.

'She had two children with him and they divorced three years ago. Mac is her second husband.'

They fell into silence for another few miles.

'Did I ever really know you?'

The softly spoken question almost tore her in half. She swiftly turned her face to the passenger window, watching with tear-filled eyes as the scenery passed by in a rainswept haze. 'I probably never let you close enough to.'

'Or I didn't ask the right questions.'

'Maybe.'

He glanced at her reflection. 'She'll be just fine when you see her, you know. Your brother-in-law would have told you if she wasn't.'

Teagan smiled a soft smile at him in the glass. 'I know. I just want to see her. Then I'll be fine too.'

There was a nod as he looked forward again.

When he went quiet Teagan found herself gathering confidence from his silent strength. Just by being there he made her feel that everything would be okay. It was something very new to her, taking strength from someone else. And it made her curious about what made up the kind of person who would give so much when they were constantly rebuffed.

And he was right. He hadn't really known her as well as he'd thought when they were younger. But it wasn't because she hadn't wanted him to. It was just that she had liked how she saw herself though his eyes. He had admired her strength, coaxed out her laughter, stimulated her mind. And under that attention she had blossomed. She hadn't wanted to be reminded of other things. So she had never allowed them to be brought up in conversation.

But it had been dishonest of her. She had owed him more than that. Still did, in a way.

More composed, she turned and studied his profile, hesitating for just a moment. 'You didn't have to do this.'

'Yeah, I did.' He smiled, his eyes still focused forward. 'I'm your knight in shining armour, remember?'

She couldn't help herself. 'Why did she let you go? Your wife?'

The smile faded at her softly spoken question. He flexed his fingers against the steering wheel. 'Are you going to use the fact that my marriage didn't work to prove your theory?'

'What?'

He didn't look at her. 'You've told me about your parents, and about Eimear's first marriage. It's all proof of your great lonely plan for life. I won't add to that, Teagan.'

The air within the car changed. 'I thought you didn't want us to argue.'

'I don't.'

'So it's all right for you to ask me questions, but not all right when it's the other way around?'

Brendan sighed, his fingers flexing and unflexing again. 'My marriage has nothing to do with you and me.'

'There isn't a "you and me".'

'Yes, Teagan.' He looked her straight in the eye for a brief, charged moment. 'There is. Whether you choose to accept it or not.'

'Just because I came to you for help again?'

'Because I was the first person you thought of.' There was a momentary break as he negotiated a turn. 'And that means something. *I* still care.'

'How can you?' she asked in astonishment. 'I haven't given you any encouragement!'

'No, not in the usual way, you haven't.' His smile was rueful. 'But one thing you said was right, I guess. I *do* see that as a challenge. I see you as challenging. Because I don't think you want to be alone, Teagan. Not really.'

Her eyes were wide as he turned and looked at her and added, 'Any more than I do.'

CHAPTER EIGHT

THEY saw Mac first. And as they walked with him along the corridor towards Eimear's room the injuries to his face from the airbag in the car made Teagan's stomach churn. But the churning abated when the door opened and her eyes fell on her sister's smiling face.

As Brendan had predicted, she was fine. Well, as fine as she could be, with a couple of cracked ribs and associated bruising.

After some talk about how it had happened, Teagan was happy her younger sibling was well. But when Eimear babbled about how much she missed her children a churning of a different kind grew.

'I can't believe you were so selfish.'

Eimear seemed to sink back further into her pillows. Eyes the exact shade of Teagan's grew wide with surprise. 'How can you say that?'

'Eimear, you went *days* without calling those kids.'

'I've just come out of a bad accident!' She shook her head in disbelief. 'Why are you being like this?'

Maybe because, having just survived the car journey from hell, to find her sister propped up in bed looking like a film star hadn't impressed her. That and a good dose of relief translated into resentment.

'You were away *days* before you had the accident, and even when you were able to ask for a phone it didn't occur to you to phone them. It would have been the first call I made.'

'Of course it would. Because you always do everything right.' A shimmer developed into two fat tears that streaked down her cheeks. 'I knew the children would be fine with you. You know how much I love them.'

Teagan paced restlessly up and down at the foot of her bed. Arguing with her sister had not been the first thing she'd thought she'd do when she saw her. But, once she'd reassured herself that she was one hundred per cent alive, things had kind of spilled over. This had been coming for a while. And all Brendan's constant pushing hadn't helped.

'You can't keep putting them second.'

'I *don't* put them second.'

'Yes, you do.' She stopped pacing, grasped the metal end of the bed and stared. 'When it comes to men, yes, you do. And that's wrong. How can you not see that?'

'I can't lose another husband, Teagan. I really can't.' Eimear's voice was pleading. 'I need to make it work so that we don't end up like Mum and Dad. You of all people should understand.'

It was a low blow, using their shared history as a weapon. 'Don't do that. We're both old enough to take responsibility for our own lives now.'

'Are we?' Her tone became sarcastic in defence. 'Is that why you arrived with some gorgeous lump of a man to support you?'

Teagan blushed a deep red. 'Leave him out of this. He's someone who has been kind enough to help with *your* children this last while. I couldn't have managed without him.'

'You always manage.'

'No, I don't, Eimear!'

Eimear seemed shocked by the outburst. 'Yes, you do. You always have.'

'Not always.' Teagan let a shaky breath escape her mouth, shaking her head as she looked away from Eimear's face and around the room at the pristine walls. 'And I'm tired of it. Really, *really* tired.'

When Eimear said nothing, she kept talking. 'I was so scared when Mac called. I just needed to see you were all right.'

'I am. But cracked ribs aren't much fun.'

'But they're still no excuse for not calling. Just for once it would have been nice if you'd thought about someone else. Thought about how people would feel when they didn't hear from you.'

'I knew you'd be worried.'

'Then you should have called!' Her frustration rose again. 'And what about before the accident? What about the days when you didn't think to call the kids even once?'

'We were in the middle of nowhere! And we needed some time alone.'

It was like talking to a brick wall. 'Not good enough, Eimear. You don't deserve those amazing kids.' She used the all too apt description that Brendan had made of them. 'Take some time and have a think about that. And about what it was like for *us* when we were their ages!'

Without waiting for a reply she turned and yanked open the door and ran down the hall. She needed air. She needed air that wasn't tainted with the awful smell of hospital disinfectant that she remembered too well from when their mother had been so ill. The memory brought a long-buried vision of a woman with a face as beautiful as Eimear's.

A woman who hadn't walked out of the hospital like Eimear would. Who would never hear all the frustration that Teagan felt as Eimear had just heard.

Suddenly Teagan needed to be away from the consuming sense of loneliness she felt. Brendan was right. For about the hundredth time. She *was* lonely.

And when she finally made it into the open air, the years of loneliness washed over her. The emotion was too strong to hold back. And the fact that she didn't have the strength to hold it back made her angry. Angry as hell.

Brendan found her outside the building, pacing up and down on the damp grass. 'Where did you disappear to?'

'I needed air.'

'Eimear looked okay.' He had only briefly stuck his head around the door and had then gone to get a cup of tea with Mac. Who seemed like a nice enough guy to him.

Teagan's laughter was sarcastic, and overly loud. 'Oh, yeah, she's just grand.'

Brendan frowned as she continued to pace. 'What happened?'

'We had a row. It seems to be all I can do these days.'

Stepping forward, he reached out a hand to halt her pacing. She in turn wrenched her arm out of his reach and swung on her heel to face him, with her eyes sparking. 'Don't. Just don't. There's no way you can possibly understand how I feel right now.'

'Not if you won't tell me.'

'Why should I tell you?'

He took a breath. 'Because you need to tell someone, that's why. You can't keep bottling all this stuff inside.'

'I've managed all this time!' Her anger rose even though she knew that what he was saying was true. 'The fact that I'm not managing right now is all your fault!'

That did it. His eyes flashed at her. 'How in hell is it *my* fault?'

'Because you just have to keep on pushing me. I was fine the way I was!'

The flashing faded and he understood. He reached again, his voice soft. 'No, you weren't.'

'Yes, I was!' Her voice cracked as she avoided his touch once more, swinging her arm out to her side. 'I was in control of my life. I didn't need help from anyone. I didn't feel like I needed to *rely* on anyone.'

His arm dropped to his side as he accepted the fact he wasn't going to get within ten feet of her. So he stood and let her get it all out.

The tears were flowing now. Many years' worth of the damn things. 'And now you've made me stand back and look at my life, and the first bloody thing I do when I see my sister in hospital is jump down her throat.'

'Tell me why.'

'Because she didn't think to call those amazing kids she has! She doesn't even realise what she has, and that kills me.'

There was an abrupt silence. Then Brendan simply blinked. 'It kills you because you *know* how much it's worth. Because you gave up any chance of ever having something that amazing so you could be alone. When that's not really what you want at all.'

The words knocked the wind from out of her sails and she stopped her pacing, rooted to the spot as she stared at him. The anger seemed to die suddenly, her wide eyes blinking. 'I gave it up because I can't deal with it. *Obviously.*' She laughed again, a harsh, self-deprecating laugh. 'I can't even deal with the one person I spent half my life caring for. I shouldn't have gone up there and given out to her.'

With the lowering of her voice he braved a step

forward and pulled her slowly towards him, his voice soft. 'Teagan, you're human. You were frightened you'd lost the only family you know, and all that did was make you spill out a lot of stuff you've been holding inside. That's all.'

She stopped when she was still at arm's length, struggling against his firm hold while her voice rose again. 'I would never have yelled at her before.'

He held her in place. 'I know you wouldn't. But there had to come a time when you told her to be responsible for her own actions. When you told her how you really felt.'

She struggled harder. 'It's you and all this damn psychoanalysis stuff! Why couldn't you just have left it alone? What difference does it make to you what way I lead my life?'

'I couldn't watch you so shut off. It's just such a waste, because you have so much in you to give if you'll just trust yourself to let someone in.' He continued to hold onto her. 'Go right on and let it all out now. Let go, Teagan.' He took a deep breath. 'Let me in.'

'I can't.' She still fought him, pulled from side to side against his hands. Until she gave up and raised her small fists to beat on his broad chest. 'I won't do this. Let me go!'

'No.'

A sob racked her body as the beating fists slowed. 'I wasn't lonely before.'

'Yes, you were. You shut yourself off from loads of people who could have cared about you if you'd just given them the chance. And not just me.'

Another sob. And her voice caught on her words. 'I don't want to need anyone.'

'I know you don't.' As the softly beating fists stilled he freed one arm to lift his hand to her head. He flattened his palm, ran it down over hair, soothing her while he pulled her closer. 'But everyone needs someone, Teagan. If it wasn't me, at some point it would have been someone else.'

As her head came to rest against his chest she took a breath. 'No one has ever pushed as hard as you have.'

He held her in silence, smoothing his hand against her hair until her breathing slowed and she sniffed loudly. Then he took a shaky breath of his own. 'I remember a different Teagan. One who wasn't so insular. One who laughed more and shared more. I'd like to see her back.'

After a few minutes Teagan raised her head, tilted it back and looked up into his face. She knew that face so well, remembered it from days when they had laughed together, talked together. It was a lifetime ago. And all she'd done since was teach herself how to shut down emotionally. She'd laughed less with each passing year.

She didn't want to be that lonely any more. Even if it was just for a little while.

Reaching a hand up from his chest, she curled it around his neck, let her fingers tangle in the coarse hair she found there. Then she tugged.

He stayed still, held himself tall. 'No.'

Her eyebrows rose in question.

'I'm not going to kiss you. That's the last complication you need right now.'

It was the very last thing she'd expected to hear him say. Dear Lord. She'd got this really wrong, hadn't she? She was that much of a mess—whereas less than a fortnight ago she'd been so in control of her world. Or so she'd thought.

Had she really mistaken an offer of friendship for something more? Had she wanted there to be something more so very much?

'It's not that I don't want to.'

So she *wasn't* actually losing her powers of intuition. *Thank heaven.* She tugged on his neck again.

Brendan lifted the hand from her hair and gently untangled her smaller hand from his neck. 'But I'm not going to here and now. I won't have you accuse me some time of taking advantage of an emotionally charged situation.'

Teagan couldn't look him in the eye, despite his smile of reassurance. She was more humiliated than she'd ever felt in her entire life. 'Forget about it.'

Allowing her to pull back against his arm, he held onto her long enough to make one final comment, 'Know one thing, though. It will happen. Just not right now.'

CHAPTER NINE

'THAT'S sorted. They had a cancellation, so we're in.' He smiled at her, his white teeth glinting in the dim light.

Raising her head, she smiled back at him. A simple, genuine smile. Then her mind put together what he'd just said. '*A cancellation?*'

'It's a twin room, so don't panic. I just hope you brought some sensible pyjamas.'

Her pulse fluttered at the thought of sharing a room with him. Even one with twin beds. There was an intimacy involved that she hadn't experienced with anyone else. Leastways, not when it hadn't been entirely on her own terms.

He didn't miss her hesitancy. 'We're not going to get anywhere else at this time of night in the middle of peak season.'

'I know.'

After a moment he looked down at the gravel at his feet, deep in thought. Then he raised his head, pinned her with his fathomless eyes and stepped towards her. Teagan pushed her body away from the car, stood a little taller, knowing in doing so that she wasn't discouraging his approach. In fact she might as well have been daring him to make a move.

She smiled a little shyly. Trying to let him see that things had changed.

When he was inches away from her he looked into her eyes and laughed a low laugh. It was a deep, rumbling sound that seemed to shake his broad chest before it made its way into the air. 'Don't go giving me that look, Teagan Delaney.'

She continued to smile back at him. 'What look?'

'Oh, you know what look. You're *flirting* with me.'

Tilting her head to one side, she blinked, her voice husky. 'I have no idea what you're talking about. I'm just glad you found a room.'

He laughed again, waggled a long finger at her. 'You're doing it again. Quit.'

With a tilt forward onto her toes, she closed the minuscule gap left between their bodies, still looking up at him with her head to one side.

'I feel like I've had the weight of the world on my shoulders.' She shrugged the shoulders under discussion. 'And now it doesn't seem so heavy any more. That's all. I guess it's *liberating*.'

The smile he gave her was affectionate, and he reached the previously waggled finger forward and gently brushed her hair back behind one ear, his fingers lingering there. 'You let a lot of stuff out. That was a big thing.'

'Yes, it was.' She blinked back at him with equally affectionate eyes. 'I'm sorry I beat you up, though.'

'It would take more than a wee slip of a thing like you to beat *me* up.'

Teagan continued to smile, before she felt the wave of shyness roll over her once more. Standing back on the flat of her feet, she looked at her favorite button on his shirt. The button at the base of his strong neck, where a steady pulse was beating.

'You okay?'

'This is just a bit strange, I guess.'

'What I find strange is that you've managed to get this far through life without anything like this ever happening before.'

'I told you. No one ever pushed this hard before.' A small scowl accompanied her blinking eyes. Then, without thinking, she raised her hand and toyed with the button, twisting it between her thumb and forefinger.

His voiced dropped to a low, intimate grumble. 'I didn't mean that part. I meant this kind of intimacy part.'

'No.' Her eyes moved slowly upward. 'I felt that one time before.'

Brendan took a moment to catch on to her meaning. When he did, the fingertips on her hair stilled and his chest rose and fell in a deep sigh. 'Last time you ran. Will you run this time too?'

'I don't want to run. I'd like to see what comes next.'

'You have a lot on your plate at the minute—'

'That's not a reason to step back, though. Is it?'

It wasn't? Brendan was having to exert every ounce of self-control he had. It was getting to be a constant inner battle when she was around. And he was only human, after all. But there was a fine line in operation here, and he knew it. He didn't want to be Teagan's 'rebound' in her emotionally suppressed life. He wanted something longer-lasting than that. And somehow he had a feeling that to lose her now would be even more painful than facing up to the fact his marriage hadn't worked.

It was going to take a little time, that was all. 'You have no idea how hard it is not to kiss you right now.'

The smile she gave him was seduction personified.

'Teagan, stop it.'

The hand on the button stilled, then rose to touch the side of his face.

His hand landed on hers, holding it against his skin. For a second he closed his eyes, let the sensation of her touch wash over him. 'I think we should get to know each other better this time.'

She continued smiling. 'Oh, so do I.'

The statement raised another small burst of laughter. 'That wasn't what I meant.' Tangling long fingers with hers against his cheek, he lifted her hand from his face, keeping their fingers entwined. 'We could do with taking things slow.'

When she raised an eyebrow in question, he added in a low rumble, 'There are other ways of being intimate.'

'There are?' Teagan was surprised at the breathless tone to her voice.

Brendan nodded, slowly and deliberately.

And her throat went dry. 'Such as?'

Tangling his fingers in and out of hers, he rubbed his thumb back and forth against the soft flesh at the base of her thumb. 'You'll have to trust me.'

That was just the thing, though. She already did, didn't she? It wasn't just a lot of old family stuff and emotional constipation she was letting go of, thanks to him. It was also her inability to trust someone who was able to touch her heart. And that was a big step. One that had been creeping up on her of late and she hadn't even noticed.

To have trusted him with the children, to have accepted his help. To have gone to him first when she had a crisis, and more than anything to have let him get to know the real her. All those things told her that trust was already in place. He was special.

'I do trust you, Brendan.'

His thumb stilled. He blinked at her for several long, heart-warming moments, and then leaned forward and pressed his warm mouth against her cool temple. He lingered there for a long time, breathed in deeply the scent of her hair, and then removed his mouth and replaced it with his forehead, his eyes looking deep into hers, up close.

Teagan smiled. She couldn't seem to stop smiling. It was one of the most intimate moments she had ever experienced with a man. And that was just from a kiss on the forehead. Where would the amazing journey take her next?

The first place it took her was to what could turn out to be a cringingly embarrassing night sharing a room with him after all that had happened. Given the choice, it might have been easier to spend a few hours away from him, to take it all in and think about what was happening.

But maybe, if she'd believed in fate, she might have thought it was a *good* thing they had to share. Because that way she couldn't run again—couldn't take a moment to step back. And even though she'd told him she wanted to see what came next, there was no guaranteeing that a little time away from him wouldn't have sent her back to the thinking that had made her run before. After all, she was working against years of old habits. She could hardly expect to change overnight.

By sharing she didn't have time to *over*-think, in the way he had so rightly accused her of doing once before. She just had to live for the moment. Experience it as it happened, without tearing it to shreds.

And even though that decision stopped her cringing, she was most definitely embarrassed. And self-conscious. And nervous. And filled with anticipation.

A lot of conflicting emotions to feel while standing in a tiny shower-room-cum-bathroom.

She finished brushing her teeth, smoothed her hands down over her striped pyjamas. And took a deep breath.

'Have you fallen down a hole?'

A smile crossed her face as his voice sounded from the other side of the door.

'I promise not to peek if you're wearing something sexy.'

Liar. She laughed softly.

'Though, just out of curiosity, *are you?*'

She laughed louder, the sound echoing off the tiled walls. 'I could just sleep in here, you know.'

There was a 'click' from just past the door, and then his voice sounded in a low grumble. 'Lights off. Come to bed.'

Oh, and just who was flirting now? After a moment's worth of calming thoughts, she opened the door and used the light from the small room to give her her bearings. She could see the dark shape of Brendan lying in the narrow bed furthest from her, but because the small arc of light fell on the foot of his bed, she couldn't quite make out what side he was lying on, or whether or not his eyes were open. Until his voice sounded again, husky in the dim light.

'You know, my switching off *this* light would have worked if you hadn't left that light behind you on. I can see lots with that light on.'

Teagan's eyes widened as she realised she was lit from behind. How much *could* he see? Her hand reached for the pull string as she simultaneously launched herself at the nearer bed.

He chuckled beside her.

After some shuffling beneath the covers the room became silent and she held her breath, listening for him. She couldn't even hear him breathing. And then he laughed as they both exhaled in unison.

'Well, this isn't at all awkward,' she whispered across at him, turning in his direction.

His bed creaked as he moved. 'It's been an eventful day, one way or another.'

'Yes, it has.'

'We should do something fun tomorrow, to balance it out, don't you think?'

The reasoning brought a smile to her face. 'Killarney doesn't have a zoo.'

'Damn.'

'We could try something else, I guess.'

'My, my, Ms Delaney, volunteering to have fun? I'm impressed.'

The edge to his low voice painted a mental image of the smile on his face for her. As she closed her eyes she could almost see it. The sparkle in his dark eyes, the laughter lines creasing on either side. His face was indelibly painted on her brain.

'You asleep?'

She continued smiling. 'No.'

'So tell me something I don't know.'

'You need more already? You've got more in a few days than most people ever get.'

His voice was laced with affection. 'I know. So let's try something simpler. Something that no one else knows about you.'

Sharing simple details. Was this another example of the intimacy he had talked about? Her heart fluttered. Lying in the darkness with a man like Brendan, talking about things that no one else knew, *was* intimate. It was sharing. It was trusting someone else. It was another validation of the things that were already there between them. The fact that he was still validating it for them both touched her.

'I brush my hair one hundred times before I go to bed.'

His laughter was throaty this time, and sounded so close that it was almost as if his head was on a pillow next to hers. 'Any bit of wonder you were in the bathroom so long.'

She laughed back. 'I read once that it was good for the scalp.'

'Mmm, a girl thing.'

'Like throw cushions?'

'Exactly like throw cushions.'

Their breathing filled the silence again. Then Teagan spoke. 'Your turn.'

'I like chocolate milk on my cereal.'

'Child.'

'I prefer to think of it as being young at heart.' He rustled his covers as he moved again. 'Your turn.'

She hesitated for a moment. 'I'm glad you came with me today. It's the first time I've been in a hospital since my mother died.'

The confession was met with another rustle. 'Give me your hand.'

She reached out in the darkness until his warm fingertips caught hers and held on. He wrapped their fingers together and ran his thumb over the sensitive skin where her pulse was beating.

'I'm glad I was there too.'

Her thumb echoed the movement against his wrist. It was enough. Just those simple words and the holding of hands. It was enough after all she'd been through in less than twenty-four hours. And for the first time in her life she felt safe.

Brendan heard her breathing deepen, felt her hand getting heavier. And he smiled again in the darkness, more hopeful than he'd felt in years.

'Teagan?' He whispered her name.

'Yes?' she whispered back, in a sleepy voice.

'If you'd worn something sexy I'd have peeked.'

She sighed, with a smile in her voice. 'I know you would have. I might even have wanted you to.'

CHAPTER TEN

FIRST thing in the morning, the continued intimacy of secret-swapping found her persuaded into one of the famous jaunting car tours of Killarney's Muckross House and gardens. Brendan had been stunned at breakfast when she had told him she'd never visited Killarney before, and had asked her just what kind of travel agent she was supposed to be. So she hadn't had a lot of choice when he had then announced his plan for fun in Killarney to balance everything else out.

But it was worth it. Teagan couldn't remember ever having so much light-hearted fun. They laughed the whole way through the trip as the jarvey, a local man who drove their car, told them tales of the area, with a good dose of Blarney thrown in for good measure.

But the thing was that their fun was more than equally interspersed with yet more moments of intimacy. Moments when Brendan would brush her hair back, or place an arm around her waist to hold her safe when the jaunting car hit a bump. Moments when she would rest her head on his shoulder as tears of laughter rolled down her cheeks, and moments when he would simply wrap his fingers with hers and hold on.

Like he did when they stepped down off the jaunting car at the rack in Kenmare Place and walked hand in hand into the town, to look for presents for the children.

He swung their joined hands gently back and forth. 'Do you want to get them something fun, or something with educational value?'

'Tough choice.' She grinned across at him. 'Though I'll bet you'll pull a face if I say educational.'

He pulled a face.

Teagan laughed. 'I knew it. We'd better get something fun then, because I don't know if I could live with that face.'

'There's nothing wrong with my face.'

'Most of the time, I'd agree.'

'You see.' He leaned the face under scrutiny a little closer to hers. 'You think I'm adorable already.'

'Oh, yeah, that's you.' She stopped in the middle of the busy pedestrian area. 'Cute as a puppy.'

The hand-swinging stopped and he reached his other hand to tangle it with hers, so that both hands were held in his grasp. Then he glanced around them at the crowds of tourists, his fair brows rising before he looked back into her eyes, his breath fanning her face. 'You're a little on the cute side yourself.'

Of all the places she'd expected to experience her second ever kiss with Brendan, the middle of a busy public street was pretty much last. But it was where he chose.

She should have learned to expect the unexpected with him.

He leaned his head down, his eyes still on hers. When her eyes widened he smiled, tilting his head so that his mouth would fit over hers. Then, less than an inch from her lips, he hesitated, quirked his brows in question, almost as if he was seeking her permission.

So Teagan closed the gap. She'd wanted to be kissed by him for such a long time that any embarrassment she might have felt about their location faded. It didn't matter where. Just so long as it happened.

All the interspersed intimate moments had built a need inside her to a point that with any other man the act itself would probably have come a poor second. But this was Brendan, whose kiss had haunted her for years.

The first touch was gentle. Warm mouth to warm mouth, firm lips to soft. The simplest joining of male to female. Then Teagan moved her head a little, pressed her mouth a little firmer, and was rewarded with a smile against her lips before he accepted the silent invitation.

He took his time with it too, tilting his head one way, then releasing the pressure enough to lift his head for a heartbeat and tilt it the other way to fit to her again. And that was how he kissed her. One touch, then a tilt of the head and a touch from another angle. Then again, and again, while Teagan felt as if a very old wound was being mended.

There was a loud wolf whistle aimed at them from a passer-by.

Pulling apart, they both laughed, and Teagan honestly felt as if she hadn't been kissed since she was twenty-one. Every other kiss faded from her memory. She shone her eyes up at him. 'I don't think I've ever been kissed in the middle of the street before.'

He pressed a firmer, smacking kiss on her mouth and whispered, 'You've not lived,' before he freed one of her hands and began to walk in step with her again.

Teagan swung their hands this time. 'Do you want to head home after we get the presents?'

'Mmm.' He glanced over at her. 'I thought you might want to go back to the hospital one more time.'

She stopped swinging. 'I hadn't actually planned on it.'

They continued walking, moving a little closer to the shop-fronts, so they could look through the large windows. Brendan tried again. 'You don't think it might be a good idea?'

Teagan stopped in front of a display of toys and sighed at her own reflection. Their morning had taken her mind off the argument with Eimear, but now it was back, like a dull headache at the back of her head. 'I don't want to row with her again.'

'Then don't.'

'I thought you just said you thought it was a good idea to go?'

'It doesn't matter what I think.' He shrugged, his gaze on her reflection in the large window. 'It's what you think that does.'

'It does matter what you think.'

He smiled in response to the softly spoken words. They'd come such a long way in a short space of time already. A leap of faith of sorts. For them both.

'I'm glad.'

Teagan smiled back at him. 'So, what *do* you think?'

With a quarter-turn he faced her and released her hand, to wrap his arms around her waist. 'I think you should go see her again and talk. Just talk. Listen to what she has to say after yesterday, and tell her how you feel a little more calmly. You'll feel better for it.'

Leaning her head back so she could look up at his eyes, Teagan played over what he'd said. She'd never asked anyone for advice when it came to Eimear. Had taken every decision alone. But he was right. Surprise, surprise.

She sighed. 'I hate you sometimes.'

'I know you do.' He leaned down and pressed another light kiss on her lips. 'Some days I don't much like me either.'

* * *

They had Eimear sitting up in a chair when Teagan opened the door to her room. She looked very beautiful, if a little ethereal in her paleness. But then she'd always been the prettier of them—the little girl with dark curls and a smile that had charmed everyone. Teagan had felt invisible beside her, the silent, serious one. The awkward tomboy who had fought every step of the way to make her beautiful sister feel safe and cared for.

Even as she stood and looked at her now she still felt like the serious one. Despite Brendan's help. The only thing that had really changed was that she didn't look like a tomboy now. And she wasn't silent any more either. Her last visit had proved that.

'Hi.' She felt truly awkward in her own sister's company for the first time in her life. And it wasn't a pleasant sensation. Had they really moved so far away from where they'd once been? It had once felt as if it was just the two of them against the world.

'Hi.' Eimear turned her head and blinked at her with wide eyes. 'I didn't think you would come back.'

'Neither did I. Brendan talked sense into me.'

'Wow. So much influence already?'

Teagan smiled a small smile. 'Apparently. He doesn't take too much of that old stubborn nonsense from me.'

Eimear nodded, her eyes straying from Teagan's face to the wide windows that dominated one side of her room. 'Mac's like that with me. I think that's why I fell in love with him.'

At the sad tone to Eimear's voice Teagan felt herself drawn into the room. Looking around for another chair, she found a standard hospital plastic version and dragged it over to sit opposite her sister. Then she leaned back in it and took a breath before she jumped in. 'So what went wrong with him?'

'It's me. I think I push people away.'

Her eyes widened in shock. Oh, no. That couldn't be right. 'But you've always been the open-hearted one.'

'You think so?' Eimear glanced back with a sad smile. 'We're not really that different, Teagan.'

'But you—'

'Had you to look out for me. Yes. I know that. And I can't look back on being a kid without knowing that it was you who loved me and cared for me. Way more than Mum and Dad did.'

Teagan felt her throat get tight. 'You were my family.'

'And you were amazing.' When Eimear turned her face full-on, tears were shimmering in her eyes. 'I just haven't done so great since I went out into the world without your influence. I was going to go out and build a proper family, the way you taught me it should be. I thought if I did then you could go out and find someone great of your own.' She took a shaky breath. 'You had so much love to give to a family of your own. It didn't seem right that I held you back.'

Tears of her own welled up. How had she not known that was how Eimear felt? And how had she failed so miserably to live up to the dream that Eimear had had for her?

It was taking Brendan to show her that such things were even a possibility.

'I'm sorry I shouted at you.'

'No, it's all right. Don't apologise.' Eimear reached a hand towards her and smiled when it was accepted. 'You were right. I love those kids so much, Teagan. I really do. They're my babies. But sometimes I really do feel like I'm not as good a mother as you were to me, and that scares me. So I rely on Mac being there to help me. Maybe too much.

And when we started having problems I focused all my energy on that, rather than trying to fix what was wrong with the way I am with my kids.'

Teagan let the tears roll down her cheeks openly as she listened. It had been so long since Eimear had shared how she felt with her. She'd never known that she'd felt she was letting her children down in some way. She *should* have known. Maybe she could even have helped. But she'd been so busy building her own life. Trying to lose herself in her work, and trying not to admit she'd been lonely. But she could try and help now.

She squeezed her fingers. 'Does he love you? Really? Properly?'

'Yes, he does. I kept pushing him to prove it, trying to make him realise how important it was. But no matter how many times he told me how much he loved me, I just wasn't convinced. It was me. I did the damage.'

'Is it better now?'

The smile, although watery, was genuine. 'Yes. We talked for hours last night. Now I just want to see our kids.' She tried leaning forward, grimaced, then slowly leaned back. 'Tell me how they are?'

Teagan wiped her cheeks with her free hand and then reached down into her bag for a tissue to pass to Eimear, before regaling her with tales of the zoo and camping in her front room.

It was a therapeutic visit for them both. Things that had been held back were being talked about for the first time. And it felt again as it had been between them when they were younger. Teagan hadn't realised how much she'd missed that.

But all the while her mind kept coming back to how they each had a self-destructive way of treating relationships.

So she made a new pact with herself. She swore there and then that she wouldn't make the same mistake as Eimear. There were lessons to be learned. She wouldn't push Brendan, or put him in a place where he was tested. Wouldn't look for something that might not even be there. It would be so unfair to him—certainly equally as bad a thing as denying how she felt about him in the first place had been.

Thing was, she was already falling for him again. Had probably fallen a good deal of the way when she was twenty-one, if she was honest. What she couldn't do was put any pressure on him. She couldn't try and force something that might not be as strong for him as it might be for her.

She would bide her time. She would wait. And when he was sure of how he felt, then she would let him know how *she* felt. She wouldn't turn into some obsessive possessive. She'd take a chance.

CHAPTER ELEVEN

'Do you ever actually work?'

'It's the beauty of working for yourself. You get to dictate your own hours.'

'Yes, I get that bit.' She tried her best to sidle past him without him reaching out to tickle her ribs. She failed, so continued on a giggle. 'But you still have to do *some* work.'

Brendan smiled at her contortions to avoid him while she made dinner. 'I work when I leave here.'

'Really? 'Til what time?'

He shrugged. 'Three or four.'

'In the morning?' Her eyes widened in surprise. 'Aren't you exhausted?'

The truth was that he *was* exhausted. But another truth was that he didn't want to be away from her for long. It seemed as if his need for her company was greater than his need for sleep. Quite possibly born of the fear that too much time away from her would give her too much time to think. And he knew where that might lead...

'I'm fine.'

Turning her back to the counter-top, she tilted her head and searched his face. 'You'll drop if you keep going at this pace.'

The smile was slow, and seeped with meaning. 'Oh, I have plenty of stamina. Don't you worry.'

Her laughter was musical.

He let his gaze wander from the top of her shining dark crown of hair, down over her arched brows and from dimple to dimple until it rested on her mouth. When he spoke his voice was husky, and not just from lack of sleep. 'I'm serious.'

'So you say.'

His eyes jerked back to meet hers. She was flirting with him again. Out and out, plain as the sparkle in her eyes, *flirting*. And suddenly he wasn't at all tired.

With a minuscule step forward he had her body pinned back against the counter. Then he moved his arms so that his palms were flat on the cool granite either side of her.

She let out a small gasp, but another quick search of her eyes told him it wasn't a gasp of fear. *Uh-uh.*

Her pupils were large and dark, her breasts rising and falling against his chest. She was turned on.

'When did you say Eimear and Mac were coming to get the kids?'

Teagan's answer was breathless. 'Day after tomorrow.'

He nodded, his eyes moving over her face again as he tilted his head closer. 'I guess we'll have to do with more of that other kind of intimacy stuff 'til then.'

There was more? Teagan wasn't quite sure she could take much more. She watched with wide eyes as he brought his head closer, his mouth wavering over hers. But when she tried to meet him halfway he tilted his head away with a sensual smile.

'Uh-uh.' He kept his mouth a mere inch from her skin as he moved his head to the neck she dutifully arched for him with a sigh. 'My rules.'

It was agony of the sweetest kind. And if this was what other people had together, then Teagan could understand why they would try for a relationship longer lasting than a few months.

His breath fanned over the sensitive nerve-endings below her ear. 'You smell good.'

Damn, but so did he. Up close, the scent of him was one of soap and faint musk. So male, so very individually him. It made its way from her nose directly to her abdomen. And she felt the spiralling grow and spread wide. *Wow.*

She cleared her throat. 'It's Lily of the Valley.'

Again his breath tingled against her skin, this time closer to where her neck curved into the hollow of her collarbone. 'Would that be perfume or...' his head lifted so that he could look into her eyes, his mouth hovering over hers again '...body lotion?'

Who'd have thought the words 'body lotion' could take on a sexual meaning? If this was his idea of intimacy lessons without, well, the more *obvious* intimacy, then she was in big, *big* trouble.

He pushed his hips in against the cradle of her stomach. And growled a very low groan as he moved his mouth past her ear.

Teagan blew out a small breath of the air she'd been holding in her lungs.

'I want you.' Again his head tilted, this time to the other side of her neck.

Oh, damn. She wanted him too. She felt her heavy head droop back as his breath worked its way up towards her ear again, where it tickled as he whispered, 'To come and meet my family this weekend.'

She froze.

'What did you just say?'

Either he ignored the change in her, or he was so wrapped up in what he was doing that he hadn't noticed. Either way, he continued his assault on her neck. 'My family. This weekend. My sister is getting married.'

Trying her best to ignore the distraction of his mouth so tantalisingly close to her skin, Teagan focused her efforts on staying calm. He couldn't be serious.

'You can't be serious.'

Brendan stilled, his breath still brushing over her neck and returning her scent to him. But his voice changed, became less of a whisper. 'Is that a problem?'

How could he not see that it was? They were still on scarily new ground for her. And although she had slipped into the role of 'intimacy' with him fairly smoothly, he had to know that it was way too early for her to be doing the meeting-his-family thing. Not that she'd ever done that with any man before. It wasn't as if families were her forte, after all.

'Brendan—'

'Don't.' His head came back into a position where he could look her in the face. 'Don't go taking a step backwards here. It's just a family do. I won't even know half the people there myself.'

She searched for her security button. But he was wearing a T-shirt as dark a blue as his eyes, so there was no escape there. Reluctantly she looked back up at him. 'Don't you think it's a bit early?'

'Teagan, I've known you longer than five minutes. We can go as old friends, if you'd prefer.' He took a breath, and jumped in. 'But I'd really like it if we went as a couple.'

They were a couple in his mind? Her heart beat a loud rhythm while she stared at him. And if they weren't a couple, then what were they? They were certainly behaving the way a couple would, and when Anne and James had handed back the children they had immediately invited them to dinner. As a couple. So it had to be the way other people were starting to see them.

It was the first step to a commitment, and Teagan knew that. Knew it as much because of the attachment she already felt to him as by the way it looked to outsiders.

But a family wedding? That was huge. To present themselves to his family as a couple would be making a silent announcement of sorts. Did he really want that so soon?

With shock she realised she *wanted* him to want it. And she had to question again how she could feel so quick an about-face after years of vowing to walk alone.

'I just don't know—'

He stepped back from her. 'Fine. Don't worry about it. It was just an idea.'

And now she'd hurt him. Maybe even given him the impression that what was happening wasn't all that important to her. Which in turn hurt *her*—because it *was* that important. She laid a hand on his broad chest as he lifted his hands from the counter. 'No. If you really want me to go, I'll go.'

It was a big thing for her to do, and Brendan knew it. The fact that she would take such a big step for him touched him. Gave him more hope to hang onto. This was closer to the Teagan he remembered of old—the one who stepped forward bravely even when she was concerned or worried. And the fact that she was prepared to do this for him, to try something difficult out of respect for what he wanted, meant there was just no way he was going to let her do it without a full confession of what she might be walking into. 'The last time I saw them all was at my own wedding.'

She had a lightbulb moment. To attend another family wedding alone would be horrific for him, wouldn't it?

Teagan understood straight away. He wasn't actually trying to tell the world they were together. He was trying to prove he wasn't alone.

Which hurt. As if she'd just been dropped from a second-floor window and had the air knocked out of her lungs. Not two days ago she'd made a vow not to look for something that wasn't there. Not to push him.

And already she was reading too much into their situation.

But she owed him something in return for how much she'd learned about herself already, didn't she? She couldn't let him go to that wedding alone.

Pinning what she hoped was a convincing smile on her face, she stepped forward and circled his neck with her arms. 'I'll go.'

Brendan let out a breath against her hair. 'Good.'

He was nervous. She'd never actually seen him nervous before, so it took a moment for her to recognise it for what it was.

She had known he was tense the minute they'd left her house. It had been there in the set of his shoulders, in the grip he'd had on the steering wheel. And no amount of small talk had seemed to help.

So she gave up on small talk. 'What are you nervous about?'

'I'm not nervous.'

'Yeah, you are.' She smiled a soft smile at him. 'You're holding onto that steering wheel for grim death.'

'I'm not nervous.' He glanced over. 'A little tense, maybe.'

'So tell me why.' Somehow she knew it was because he was going to have to relive a different wedding. But she wanted him to be able to talk it through.

'You haven't met my family before.'

'You're nervous for *me*?' She smiled. 'I'm nervous enough for myself, don't you worry.'

The second glance he gave her was more serious. 'Do you want to go back?'

Yes. 'No.'

He looked as if he didn't completely believe her. 'Fibber. But I'm glad you're coming with me.'

One large hand reached away from the gearstick and enclosed her smaller hand, where it lay in her lap. With the back of his hand then resting against her thigh, he squeezed her fingers tightly. 'They'll like you—if you'll let them.'

Trying to ignore the warm hand against her thigh, Teagan concentrated on talking. 'Tell me a bit about them, then. I'll never remember who everyone is if there's a ton of them.'

'I thought a corporate travel agent would be good with names.'

'Names I can do, in groups of ten or less. My forte lies with matching the company with the venue.'

'Ah.' He aimed a more relaxed smile at her before loosening his hand to change gear. 'Well, the venue is taken care of this time.'

She curled her hand in her lap again, feeling a chill without his warm touch. 'So let's have a go at some names.'

'You don't need to worry about that. They'll all rush over to introduce themselves. You may well be crushed in the stampede.'

'That's right. You make me feel better about it.'

Deep laughter filled the car. 'Sorry.'

Well, at least he wasn't so tense any more. She smiled when he changed gear again, and reclaimed her hand. 'How many are we talking about, here? I mean, should I have worn running shoes?'

'Probably.' Another glance at her face brought another burst of laughter. 'They can be a tad over the top.'

'What does that mean, exactly?'

Long fingers reached out and squeezed her hand. 'Stick close to me and we might just get through.'

He might not be tense any more. But suddenly Teagan was petrified.

CHAPTER TWELVE

'OH, MY gracious! Well, it's about time.' A tall, elegant woman, with grey hair in an equally elegant twisted up-do, launched herself on them at the door. 'Hello, my darlings!'

Teagan froze as the woman engulfed her in a hug before kissing her on both cheeks. 'You must be Teagan. I'm Louisa—Brendan's mother. How lovely you look. Come in, come in.'

Blinking across at Brendan, she was rewarded with a grin over his mother's shoulder. 'Hi, Mum.'

His mother detached herself long enough to tap his shoulder and scold, 'You never visit,' before she turned, linked her arm with Teagan's and guided her firmly along the long hall of one of the largest houses Teagan had ever been in. 'He never visits any more. You must sort that out for me, dearest.'

Teagan turned her head, looked over her shoulder and pleaded for help with her eyes. Brendan simply continued to grin. The rat.

There was a thunder of feet on stairs and three laughing women appeared. 'Brendan!'

'Hi.' His voice sounded from behind Teagan. 'Shouldn't you three be dressed by now? I heard there was something on today.'

'Very funny.' One of the women fought her way to the front with a warm smile. 'You must be Teagan. I'm Allie, Brendan's sister, and I'm the one getting married. I'm so glad you could come.'

Teagan found herself hugged again. And then again. And then again, as each woman stepped forward. Her cheeks began to ache from forcing a smile. While spirited away from Brendan's sisters as they were chased off to get dressed, it occurred to her that she still hadn't spoken. She should really say something.

'You have a lovely home, Mrs McNamara.'

Louisa tapped her arm. 'Oh, shush. It's Louisa. It is lovely, isn't it? I'm very proud of it. So much easier to keep now that so many of the children are grown and away, you know. But when they lived here...' She rolled her eyes. 'Good heavens, you could barely find a chair that wasn't covered in mess enough to sit on. Absolute organised chaos.'

Teagan fought hard to keep up with how quickly she spoke. But manage she did, and she found herself smiling a more genuine smile. How could she not, around someone so openly warm? 'I can imagine.'

'And as for Brendan—well, his room nearly needed a mountaineering course to get through it, I can tell you.'

This time when Teagan glanced over her shoulder he was rolling his eyes in the exact way his mother just had.

'Now, come and meet the rest of the children. They can't wait to meet *you*. We've all been saying it was high time he went out and met some nice girl again. Just because it all went so horribly wrong last time, it doesn't mean he shouldn't try again—does it, dear?'

'Erm—'

'It's more than time. No man is an island. Don't you agree?'

Teagan had a feeling she'd heard that one somewhere before. Another backward glance and she felt her heart twist at the look of anguish she thought she caught a brief glimpse of.

But his mother kept going. 'Rebecca was a lovely girl. A computer expert, like Brendan—though I'm sure you already know that.' She sighed dramatically. 'But just not for our Brendan at the end of the day. These things happen. It's sad, though. We were all terribly upset for him.'

In the space of about five minutes she'd been handed more information about Brendan's marriage than she'd gleaned in the time since they'd got closer. And although she'd wanted to know what had happened, the fact that the information was being imparted at three times normal speaking speed, and right in front of Brendan himself, just didn't sit well with Teagan.

Louisa loosened the grip on her arm, stepping through a doorway ahead of them. 'The boys are all in here. Come right ahead. It's all a bit mad here today, I'm afraid. But we'll have time to talk later. You can tell me all about how Brendan won you over.'

Teagan hung back until Brendan was beside her. Then she glanced up at his face, her eyes taking in the tension in his jaw-line. She lowered her voice to a soft whisper. 'Should have worn those runners.'

He turned his face towards her and grinned, his eyes sparkling affectionately. 'Sorry.'

Reaching her hand over, she tangled her fingers tightly with his. Taking and giving comfort from the simple contact. 'Just don't go anywhere. Even if I say I need the bathroom.'

The hand in hers gave a gentle tug, holding her from the open doorway long enough for him to plant a kiss on her jaw-line, just below her ear, where he whispered, 'I promise.'

The hour before they left for the church became a blur of faces and information to her. The McNamara family membership was seemingly unending. Teagan wasn't convinced that if there were a questionnaire later she'd do too well.

However, she was fairly convinced her name was now *'You must be Teagan.'*

What had it been like, growing up with so much warmth and open love? To someone like a young Teagan it might have seemed like heaven. But really, judging by how Brendan reacted to the many matter-of-fact statements made about his personal life, it hadn't been that easy.

It didn't get any better at the church.

'Brendan, how lovely to see you. We were so sorry to hear about Rebecca.'

'Brendan! You're looking much better than the last time I saw you.'

Or, accompanied with a wink, 'I see you're over your broken heart, then. Who might this be?'

And even those relatives were more sensitive than the ones who just showered him with hugs and understanding looks. One elderly aunt even wept when she saw him with a new 'young girl'.

Teagan wanted to slap them all silly and smuggle him away. Instead she held onto his large hand the entire time, and smiled until she thought she'd never have the energy to smile again.

Side by side in a long wooden pew, they had their first moment 'alone'. Brendan pulled their joined hands into his free hand and leaned close to her ear to whisper, 'At least now we get a break.'

She smiled softly at him, lowering her voice to a similar whisper. 'Are you all right?'

'Me?' His fair brows rose momentarily in surprise. 'I'm fine. I'm the one that's used to all this.'

'Are you?'

The whispered question made him search her eyes. What he saw there made him glance away. She was concerned, warm, sensual, all in the one glance. And it took his breath away.

He took a moment to smile at another relative who had turned round to wave at him, then looked down to where his hands held hers. 'They all mean well in their own way.'

'Where I come from, it's called rubbing your nose in it.'

'No.' He shook his head, his eyes still on their hands. 'If they thought I thought that then they'd be very hurt. It's okay—really.'

Teagan waited until he'd raised his chin and given her a reassuring smile. 'Well, it's not okay with me.'

The smile changed to one of open affection. 'Just as well I have you here to look out for me, then, isn't it?'

Her annoyance at his family faded under the depth of his smile. She looked into the dark blue pools of his eyes, at his thick lashes blinking slowly at her. And she felt lost and found in the space of a heartbeat.

He leaned closer. 'I'm glad you came.'

Her answer was a breathless whisper. 'Me too.'

The organist sounded the first strains of 'The Wedding March' and they stood up, still hand in hand, to watch Allie make her way down the aisle on her father's arm. And they stayed hand in hand for the entire ceremony.

Teagan had no idea why she found herself so affected by it all. It wasn't as if it was the first wedding she'd ever attended. But even Eimear's two weddings hadn't had such an emotional pull for her.

But by the time a soloist stood to sing a love song she

was a goner. She felt Brendan's fingers squeeze hers and she looked up into his face, smiling at him with shimmering eyes. Then she laughed a silent laugh at her own reaction.

He smiled back, released her hand, circled her shoulders with his arm and pulled her closer to his side.

The touch of his lips against her hair was so light she could have imagined it. But she knew in her heart it had happened.

Just as surely as she knew she was in love with him.

CHAPTER THIRTEEN

WHEN Brendan had first thought about inviting Teagan to meet his family he hadn't intended to hide behind her. They were simply the people he cared about and he wanted them to meet someone else he cared about.

He also wanted her to see that not all families were like hers had been. Though that had backfired on him somewhat. It should have occurred to him that to someone new his family life would seem like an entirely different method of torture. But then, no family was perfect.

The thing about his was that he knew they were there for him. They always had been. Even if their method of showing love and affection was to talk out loud and at length about things that had been difficult.

All right, so a lesser man might have wanted to show he wasn't sad and alone by bringing someone to the wedding. But Teagan wasn't just a random date or camouflage.

She was *Teagan*.

And now, at the reception, she was fielding his family from the subject of his failed marriage like a pro.

He grinned broadly as she systematically charmed the pants off each and every one of them.

'It's nice to see Brendan looking so well again.'

His aunt Liz opened her mouth to add more, but Teagan was too quick. 'Isn't it, though?' She wrapped an arm around his waist and smiled broadly at the older woman. 'I've heard so much about all of you—I just couldn't wait to meet you. I'm so sorry.' She blinked madly. 'I didn't catch your name.'

'I'm Liz—Brendan's aunt on his mother's side.' She paused for a breath.

Brendan choked down a burst of laughter. That had been a mistake.

'Lovely to meet you.' She thrust out a hand. 'I'm Teagan Delaney. Isn't this just the loveliest wedding? I thought Allie looked gorgeous. And those dresses! It was just so beautifully done, don't you think? This has to be the biggest wedding I've ever been to.'

Aunt Liz seemed momentarily stunned. But, like every other member of his family who had been dazzled up close by the bright new star in their midst, she immediately warmed to her.

'Wasn't she lovely? She's worked so hard to have everything so nice, and with a full-time job too.' She released Teagan's hand, but didn't make the mistake of pausing for breath this time. 'I just don't know how she managed. We always have huge weddings. Why, when Brendan and—'

'That's a lovely hat, Liz. Wherever did you find such a good match for your dress?'

After another five minutes of girl talk, Brendan finally interrupted. He didn't think he could hold back the laughter for much longer. 'Auntie Liz, you don't mind if I steal a dance with Teagan, do you?'

'Brendan, of course I don't.' She reached up on tiptoes to kiss his cheek and hiss loudly, 'She's lovely. You hang onto this one, now, won't you?'

'I'll do my best.' He planted a matching kiss on her

cheek and then dragged Teagan away. It took two strides before he broke down and started laughing aloud.

'What's so funny?'

'You're amazing.' He steered them through the crowd to the packed dance floor. 'You really are.'

'And that's funny?'

When their feet hit wood he whirled her around once, and then again. Until finally he hauled her against the length of his body. 'You're out-talking my family. I didn't think that was possible.'

Teagan grinned up at him. 'Works, though, doesn't it?'

'Indeed it does.'

She swiped at his shoulder with her hand before resting it there. 'I keep trying to tell you what a highly intelligent woman I am.'

'I already knew.'

Their bodies settled into a synchronised swaying in time to the music and Teagan smiled up at him as she realised how easily it had happened. No awkwardness. No taking time to adjust to each other. They just fitted. As if they'd been dancing together for years.

'So, do you want to tell me about Rebecca yourself, or should I just let the rest of your family tell me?'

His body stiffened and he missed a step, his arm closing tighter around her waist to steady her. He glanced down at their feet for a second, before resuming a smoother rhythm.

Teagan smiled a soft, encouraging smile. 'Talking is a two-way street, I'm told.'

But when he replied his voice was cool. 'Yes, I guess it is.'

The guilt crossed her face in a wave. And it was almost as if it seeped through from her to him as he looked her in the eye. It was only natural she was curious after all she'd heard so far.

'I'm sorry. That was badly done.' She avoided his steady gaze.

It took a while of swaying and a change of background music before Brendan spoke again. She was right, after all. The talking thing *was* a two-way street. And if he wanted their delicate relationship to grow then he knew it would mean letting her in—in the same way she was trying so hard with him.

'Aunt Liz was right. The wedding was very like this one, with a lot of the same faces.'

Green eyes swept to his face again, widening with a hundred questions. 'How did you meet?'

'She was a systems analyst with the company I worked for before I went out on my own.'

'The one you went to straight after university?'

'Yes.' He smiled as he realised that she had known where he went. 'Keeping tabs on me, were you?'

Her cheeks turned a faint shade of red. 'No. Shannon mentioned it once.'

'You still keep in touch with her?'

'We talk a few times a year—do lunch when she's in town. I can give you her number, if you like.'

When her face turned away from his eyes he held her a little closer. He didn't want to name what he'd heard in her voice as jealousy, but he would love it if it was.

'Nah, I like the company I keep right now.'

This time she smiled. And he smiled back.

'So.' She tilted her head back a little. Though not quite as much as she was usually forced to, due to the height of the heels she was wearing. 'Did you date long before you got married?'

'Not long enough, as it turns out.'

'Were you very much in love with her?' It was a question that almost tore her in half. But she needed to know. Not once during the day had any member of his family had a bad thing to say about the now famous Rebecca. And even though Teagan had managed to distract herself by fielding his family away from comments that involved her, it hadn't stopped her from noticing. Or from being more than a little jealous of the woman they had all thought so much of for a while.

The music came to an end, and couples around them gradually drifted from the dance floor while the band took a break.

Brendan held onto Teagan while a million memories rattled around inside his head, his eyes focusing on hers while he thought. He watched the lights reflecting in their depths, deepening the green until they had as many facets as the precious stone they so closely resembled. And he knew the answer to her question so clearly, so suddenly, that it almost knocked him back off his feet. He should have known before. 'That was just it, Teagan. I don't know that I was.'

She stared at him with wide eyes. Obviously shocked.

He looked past the shock and over her face, so close in front of his. *How* had he not known this before? How had he not realised the crux of why his marriage hadn't worked? He had thought at the time that everything was falling into place. That he was meant to be with Rebecca and they would have a long life together. Have the family of his own that he'd always thought he would have. And now that he knew the truth he felt like dirt. He should never have married her.

He'd been very, *very* wrong.

'I didn't love her enough to fight the way I should have

to save the marriage. So she walked. And quite frankly I don't blame her.'

Now that he understood the reason he hadn't fought as hard as he should have, he *couldn't* blame her.

With a downward glance he stepped back from Teagan, released her from his arms and looked over his shoulder at the empty dance floor. 'I'm going to go and check the rooms we booked. I'll be back in a while.'

'I thought you made a promise to guard me even if I wanted to go to the bathroom?'

She was attempting to break the tension. He could see that. But he needed a little minute away from her to digest what he'd just admitted to himself. He pinned a smile to his face. 'Honey, from what I've seen, you're doing just fine with them.'

'They're not that bad.'

'Yeah, they like you too.'

'I'm glad.'

It was exactly the breakthrough he'd hoped for when he'd brought her to the wedding. He should have been chuffed to bits that she was opening up and letting people in. He should have stepped forward to show her in no uncertain terms what her fitting into his family meant to him.

He couldn't.

'I won't be long.'

When he turned to walk away her soft voice held him back. 'Why did you want me to come to this wedding with you?'

Brendan stopped. Turned. Stepped back to her. 'Why do you *think* I invited you?'

'It wouldn't have been easy to come to another wedding alone when they still talk about yours. I just want you to know that I understand that.' She shrugged. 'I guess I just need you to know I'm on your side.'

Damn it. She thought *that* was why? After all she'd shared with him the last few weeks, the intimacy that had grown between them? She really didn't know him at all.

It told him in no uncertain terms that they still had a long way to go before he could tell her what he now knew.

But he left her with a simple answer and a shake of his head. 'That's not the reason.'

'That's not the reason.'

The words played over and over in her mind while she sat in front of the large dressing table in her hotel room. It was a beautiful room, complete with four-poster bed. But the décor was wasted on Teagan as she ran a brush through her hair.

'That's not the reason.' It was almost as if she could hear his voice saying it in the room.

He hadn't explained it any further than that. Had simply looked her in the eye, then turned and walked away. Yes, he had come back again. But by that time she'd already been surrounded by his family, and the rest of the evening had gone by in a blur, until she'd once again been surrounded with hugs and kisses and loud voices vying to be heard as they all wished her goodnight.

And even though she'd never before felt such a sense of warmth and belonging, she'd also been overwhelmingly aware of the change in Brendan.

Asking him about Rebecca had been a major mistake. What *had* she been thinking? Maybe the simple truth was that she hadn't been thinking much beyond her own curiosity and jealousy? Who was the mystery woman who had captured his heart enough for him to have married her? Why hadn't it worked? Because what sane woman who had Brendan would want anyone else?

If he had wanted to tell her about it he would have. In

his own time. In his own way. And she really believed that he would have. Could have. She'd have listened. Surely he knew that?

The brush stilled in mid-air and she stared at her face with wide, unblinking eyes. *Did* he know that?

Did he know that she would be there for him in the same way that he had been for her? That was what people did for people they cared about.

'*That's not the reason.*'

That was why he had brought her to meet his family, wasn't it? He had brought her because he cared about her. And maybe, just possibly, her heart wished, because he had wanted them to see that?

Without taking the time to wonder what people might think if they found her in the elegant halls of the huge country hotel in only her nightdress, she headed for Brendan's room. She just needed to see him.

She just needed to be with him.

CHAPTER FOURTEEN

WHEN he opened the door he stared at her for a long time. Then he glanced up and down the hallway and took her hand to pull her inside. 'What's wrong?'

Teagan's eyes took in the fact that he hadn't changed. His jacket was thrown over the back of a chair and his tie was gone. But apart from loosening the buttons of his white shirt he was still dressed.

While she was in her nightdress. A Jane Austen–type number in floating silk material, no less.

She folded her arms across her breasts and tried to distract herself from a sudden wash of self-consciousness by looking around the room. It was pretty much the same as hers. Just a different colour.

'Teagan?'

Her eyes flittered back to his again. She looked at his fair hair, standing in varying spikes as if he'd been running his fingers through it. Damn, but he looked good.

His voice was soft. 'What is it?'

Rehearsing what she was going to say to him might have been an idea.

Concern filled Brendan's handsome face as he stepped forward, one hand reaching out to touch the side of her waist. 'What's wrong?'

There wasn't any point in speaking. She didn't want to speak. She could show him how she felt in other ways. Sometimes it just wasn't words that were needed.

So, self-consciousness disappearing into the warm air, she stepped forward and kissed him. She didn't touch him with her hands, didn't attempt to pull him closer. Just mouth to mouth.

He had been a good teacher. She smiled inwardly as a furtive imagination she hadn't even known she possessed slipped into gear. Maybe it was time she gave as good as she had been given.

Moving her head, she skimmed her mouth over his, touched from edge to edge. Then, with a small smile, she lifted her head an inch, tilted to the other side and repeated the process. Just as he'd done with her on that street in Killarney.

Brendan stayed still, like a rock in a storm. Only the increased rise and fall of his chest gave any indication he was even affected by what she was doing.

So she followed the path he had taught her in her kitchen, her mouth lifting from his to trail soft touches along his jaw to the skin below his ear. The scent of his musk-based aftershave was stronger as she made the kiss firmer, a completely original move of her own. Then she opened her mouth and flickered the tip of her tongue against his vaguely salty skin.

Brendan groaned. *'Teagan—'*

'Shhh.' She smiled as her softly hissed whisper of breath raised goosebumps on his skin. 'My rules.'

He groaned again, his hands rising to grip her waist. But Teagan simply continued her assault on his neck, going up on tiptoes to reach the skin behind his ear. She placed her hands on his when he pushed his thumbs into a tighter hold.

Prising his hands away, she placed his arms back by his sides, slowly lowering herself back off her toes as she worked her way down his neck.

'Teagan, stop.'

At the collar of his shirt, she nudged with her nose, exposing more skin.

'Teagan. Please stop.' His voice was husky, his body held tall and stiff. 'I'm not going to do this.'

Teagan raised her head enough to speak an inch above her favourite button. The button she had every intention of undoing. 'Who asked you to do anything?'

'Stop.'

His arms twisted swiftly, and before she knew what he was doing he had her wrists trapped and was pulling her back from his body. His husky voice whispered a firm, *'Stop.'*

Fiercely determined dark eyes watched as her chin rose. 'Why?'

'We can't do this. Not yet. It's too soon.'

'You can't hide behind my emotional state this time.' She knew with a certainty born of recent experience that he wasn't immune to her. This shared intimacy was just that. *Shared.* 'So what is it?'

He hesitated.

'Tell me.'

The fact that she had never seen him at a loss for words frightened her to death. Whatever it was, it was a big deal. And she had the sinking feeling that it was a problem *she* had created. 'I should never have asked you about her, should I?'

His breath caught.

She was right. The woman was like a spectre that hung over her—had been all damn day. 'There's been something wrong ever since. It still hurts you to talk about it.'

While she watched the inner struggle written across

his face she made up her mind to help him, as he'd helped her. To put her own jealousy to the back of her mind and focus on what he needed. She just couldn't bear to see the look of torture in his eyes. And while he remained silent she took a chance. 'You don't have to talk about it yet if you don't want to. I just want to be with you, that's all.'

The hold on her wrists loosened a degree. 'Why?'

Lord help her, it was on the tip of her tongue to tell him why. But she had to stop herself. She wouldn't push him into a place where he felt he had to voice a sentiment that he might not feel yet. Or, even worse, he might not feel what she felt and would feel he had to let her down gently.

He obviously wasn't over his marriage to Rebecca. It was too soon. Just as it would have been too soon for *her* if he'd let something happen before now. She just had to use the same self-restraint and give him the time he needed. At least he now knew that it wasn't her holding them back.

The large hands holding her relaxed again, his thumbs grazing back over the twin pulses that beat in her wrists. When he asked her again his voice had the same husky edge it had had when she was kissing him. 'Tell me why.'

Swallowing the hard lump that had formed in her throat, she smiled and admitted as much as she would allow herself to. 'Because I don't want either of us to feel lonely any more.'

'Damn it, Teagan.' He let the frustration out in his voice. 'You just have to keep on making this tough for me, don't you?'

'How am I making it tough? I'm practically throwing myself at you!' She didn't get how he could be angry with her because of that.

'That's what's *making* this so tough. I don't want to push

you away, and I don't want to make love to you if it means complicating this more than it already is.'

'Do you want me?'

'Teagan—' There was an edge of warning to his voice as his hands tightened again. 'Don't ask me stupid questions.'

Anger was the one thing that Teagan could deal with well. She'd had years of practice at being angry, so his anger wasn't going to back her down. 'And I damn well want *you*. So tell me exactly how there's a problem?'

Brendan's eyes took in the sparks of anger in hers, the flush on her cheeks, the rise and fall of her breasts beneath the scooped neck of her nightgown. He'd never been so turned on in his entire life. Had never ached so badly.

How was any guy supposed to look at her when she looked like that and not make love to her?

'Well?'

Her head cocked to one side in a challenge, dark brows arching.

He fought fire with fire. 'You're going to stand there and tell me that all that time you were so determined to go it alone has been blown away by a few weeks of intimacy with me? Or are you still trying to convince yourself?'

She practically flinched. 'You son of a—'

'Don't you dare. You've met my mother.'

'Why are you being like this?'

His jaw clenched and unclenched.

'You're fighting me when you don't want to because I hurt you earlier, aren't you?'

'You didn't hurt me!'

'Then what *is* this?' She struggled to free her arms, but when he simply held her tighter she clenched her teeth. 'You think I don't know how this works? You think I don't know what it's like to be angry because I can't face up to the fact that something hurts? You think it's easy for me to admit the fact that you're the first person I've ever wanted to try this hard to hang onto?'

Fighting himself was tough enough. Fighting her as well was too much. He hauled her forward and let out all of his frustration in one kiss. Trying to show her what he couldn't put into words yet. Ravaging her mouth with his while knowing she would probably fight him off now. She was certainly angry enough.

But she didn't. Instead she met raw, pent-up passion with passion of her own. What fight she had went into trying to free her wrists. So they struggled and kissed and twisted their bodies closer together and kissed. Until they wrenched apart, and the sound of heavy breathing filled the silent room.

It took several long minutes for their breathing to ease while they stared at each other. Then Brendan told her in a calmer voice, 'I'm still not going to make love to you. Get that clear. It's too soon.'

She struggled again. 'Then damn well let me go.'

'I don't want to let you go.'

It was the soft sincerity of the statement that made her stop struggling and listen.

'What I want is to take you to that big bed over there and hold you.'

She felt her feet propel her backwards as he pushed her body towards the edge of the four-poster.

'Just hold you. That's all I'm going to do. And when I've spent the night holding you in my arms maybe you'll realise that that's way more intimate than making love to you.'

The deep mattress hit the back of her knees. He released her wrists, placed his hands on her waist and lifted her onto the covers.

His eyes stayed locked to hers. 'I'm only human, Teagan. I may touch you, because I won't be able to stop myself. But I won't make love to you.'

Why couldn't she say something? She should say something smart or cutting, something to take him off his arrogant high horse. Who was he to push her around like this? Why did he get to make all the decisions?

He leaned in, slid his body onto the cover beside her, 'If this is going to work, in the kind of long-term, meaningful way that you've spent most of your life avoiding, we need to go slow. And that way, when we do make love, it'll be the best experience of our lives.'

The kiss was a soft caress, a promise of sorts. It ripped a hole in her chest. She didn't want to go slow.

Then he moved his mouth next to her ear and whispered, 'Slow can be good too. Trust me.'

CHAPTER FIFTEEN

WORK. It had been her hiding place for most of her life and it felt good to be back in it again. And the backlog on her desk was the most gorgeous thing she had ever seen.

When she was working she didn't have time to dwell over little things like being in love. Completely, utterly and irrevocably in love.

Unfortunately she cleared her damn backlog in the space of one day.

Which meant she ended up looking into space by six, mooning over everything that had happened in Brendan's hotel room. Playing the scene over and over in her head in slow motion. Instead of doing the obvious and heading home to persuade him to participate in more of the same torture. To try and get across to him the fact that she was *ready*.

Ever since that night she'd been a twenty-four-hour, walking version of ready. So much so that she was fairly sure she might scream out loud in frustration.

To hell with it.

She gave up on the idea of looking for any more work that needed to be done and decided instead to visit Eimear for a while before she went home. Anyway, Brendan was off up the country, catching up on some of his freelance work, so there was no rush. She needed something to distract her for a while from her state of readiness. And the only thing she could think of was the other emotion she'd been feeling of late.

She really, *really* missed the children.

When she got there they landed on her at the door with only slightly less force than Brendan's family had. 'Whoa, guys. Steady, you'll knock me off my feet.'

'Did you bring Brendan?' Johnnie tried looking past her. 'Is he here?'

'No, not today, honey. Maybe next time.'

Katie's eyes sparkled with excitement. 'Can we make tents, Auntie Teagan?'

'No, you cannot make tents.' Eimear leaned over their heads to plant a kiss on Teagan's cheek. 'Come on in. This is a lovely surprise.'

Teagan smiled at the warm greeting. There had been a lot of healing between them since the hospital, and the short visit they'd had when Eimear had collected the children. It felt good to have her sister back. And a sister she could have as a friend. 'How are you feeling?'

'Still a bit stiff, but better.' Eimear grinned over her shoulder as the children hung onto Teagan's hands. 'They've done nothing but talk about staying at your house, you know. They loved it.'

'Then they'll have to come stay again.'

The children bounced up and down at her sides, raising a squeal of excitement from the high chair by the kitchen table. 'Can we, Mummy? Can we?'

'Auntie Teagan needs a rest after last time, don't you think?'

Teagan looked up from where she'd been cooing at

Meghan, smiling down at the other two. 'Well, it was tough. But how about…' she kneeled down to their eye-level '…you promise to keep your rooms tidy for your mum and then we'll see about another visit before you go back to school?'

'I'm gonna go tidy my room!'

Eimear laughed as they thundered upstairs. 'That'll take them 'til the end of the summer, you know. I'd say you're safe enough for a while.'

'I'm serious. I'd love them to come stay again.' She pulled up a chair next to Meghan. 'Just a bit of warning this time would be good.'

'You really don't have to, Teagan. I know how busy you are.'

'I'll make time. I miss them.'

Eimear studied her head as she spooned some mashed potato into Meghan's open mouth. 'There's something different about you.'

'I had my hair trimmed.'

'No, it's not that. Though that is nice too.' She smiled. 'You've never volunteered to have the three horrors stay before. I've always had to ask.'

Teagan blushed as she glanced across at her. 'And that was very wrong of me. I aim to make up for it.'

'You should have had some, you know. They really did love staying with you, and you'd have made a great mum.'

Avoiding her smiling face, Teagan concentrated hard on getting more potato into Meghan. 'I haven't quite hit menopause yet.'

The statement was greeted with silence.

She glanced from the corner of her eye. 'What?'

'Okay. Who *is* this guy?'

She blushed again. 'What guy?'

'Oh, you know what guy. How long have you been seeing him that you're thinking about kids all of a sudden?'

'I didn't say I was thinking about having kids *now*.'

'No, you didn't, but neither did you say, "I'm too busy for kids." Which is your usual answer.' She leaned her arms across the table. 'He's serious, isn't he?'

'I don't know if he is.'

'Liar.'

'Eimear—'

She grinned broadly. 'Are you serious about him?'

Teagan swallowed hard. Maybe that was part of the reason she had come to see her sister. After all, who else was she going to talk to that stood a rat's chance of understanding what a big thing it was for her?

She blushed. 'Yes, I think I am.'

Eimear squealed so loudly that Meghan stared at her with saucer eyes. 'Sorry, baby.' She patted a pudgy arm and handed her a plastic spoon. 'Here, decorate your chair for Mummy.' Then she looked back at Teagan with sparkling eyes. 'This is amazing!'

'I'm not talking to you about this if you're going to squeal again. I mean it.'

'No squealing. I promise. Tell all.'

Where did she start? What she wanted was for someone to tell her how she should be feeling. What it was like to build something longer-lasting than the controlled relationships she'd had before.

She just needed some kind of reassurance that she wasn't going to mess it all up by doing something really stupid.

What she also needed was for Eimear to tell her there was no reason for her to feel so jealous of a woman who was quite obviously out of Brendan's life. That she shouldn't keep on being paranoid that he wasn't over her when he'd already stated he didn't think he'd been very much in love to begin with. That there was no reasonable reason why she should have a little voice in the back of her mind that said there was something he was holding back from her.

But suddenly she felt really moronic for wanting to ask any of it. So she didn't. 'I knew him a long time ago.'

'You've never mentioned him before.'

'It didn't go so well the first time.'

'But it is now, right? That's so amazing!' Eimear grasped a hand across the table and squeezed hard. 'It's what I've always wanted for you.'

Teagan smiled. 'It's still fairly early days, though.'

Another squeeze. 'This needs coffee and biccies to celebrate.' She got up from the table and started to fill the kettle, her back to Teagan. 'I'm so glad I was nice to him when I saw him today now.'

Teagan's eyes bored into her back. 'You saw him today?'

'Oh, yeah. I was shopping with Meggie on O'Connell Street and we stopped for some lunch.'

He had said he would be up the country all day. Why would he lie about that? Teagan shook her head. Already she was acting like a possessive girlfriend. That would help things along. There must have been a last-minute change in plans, that was all.

'Meggie cooed at him when we walked by their table. I thought it was so cute.' She switched on the kettle and reached for mugs, her back still to Teagan.

'That's 'cos you just *wuv* Brendan, don't you, sweetie?' Teagan smiled affectionately at her niece.

'God, it really is as well I was nice. When I saw him with that gorgeous woman I thought the worst.'

Gorgeous woman?

'He looked so embarrassed too.' Eimear laughed, 'Poor woman. I gave her the most evil eye when he introduced us.'

Introduced? Her stomach sank to her feet as foreboding washed over her. 'What was her name?'

'Rebecca something…'

This was exactly the reason she had avoided falling for someone before, wasn't it?

It had been years since she'd experienced the gaping open wound in the chest sensation she was feeling by the time she got home.

And she hadn't even wanted to *go* home, which made her feel worse. Her home was her sanctuary, the one place she'd worked to have that was for her and her alone. But with Brendan across the road she now wanted to avoid it. Which made her hate him even more than she already did for the sense of betrayal she felt.

How could he?

Or, more to the point, how could *she*? How could she have believed in him so quickly?

By the time she was inside her house she had no choice but to admit that it was because she had wanted to. She had *wanted* to believe that it was possible for her. Even though she decided it *wasn't* for her she had wanted to believe it was *possible*.

That there was still a little magic out there, somewhere.

Now she knew she'd been right to stay the way she'd been before he'd wandered back into her life. Now she knew she'd been as wrong to ignore the little voice in her head about Rebecca as she had been back in the day under that bloody mistletoe, when her voice had said, 'Oh, no.' Oh, now she knew, all right.

Trouble was, it was too late. Because she'd already humiliated herself by practically throwing herself at him.

She'd already opened herself up to heartache by trusting in him. She'd already made the damned open wound exist by loving him.

And she now hated his guts, for all of those things.

She went straight upstairs and stood under the shower, scrubbing and scrubbing at her skin as if it would remove any trace of him. But she didn't shed a tear. She wouldn't allow herself to.

Once she was dressed in her most worn pair of jeans and a long, comfort sweater of thick Aran knit, the doorbell rang.

She let it ring. But after the fourth ring she knew it had to be Brendan. Who else was likely to come to her door after nine at night?

Who else would have thought they could, without ringing first? Felt they had that right because of *intimacy*?

She stood on her side of the door and breathed in and out. And in and out. Forcing back anger until the doorbell rang again. And when she yanked it open it was exactly who she'd thought it would be on the other side. Leaning against the brick wall looking gorgeous, and bearing a pizza box and a bottle of wine. 'Hi.'

Teagan's chin rose.

'I have a load of work to do, Brendan.'

'You still need to eat, though.' He kept smiling while his eyes searched hers.

'I've eaten.'

'Well, then, you can keep me company while I eat.' He stepped forward, his smile fading when she blocked his way.

'I don't think so.'

It didn't take a mastermind to work out she was angry. And he had a fairly good idea as to where that anger came from. He had come over prepared to deal with it. But what caught him off guard was that she was cold as hell, which was even more worrying. Anger he could have dealt with. He'd dealt with it from her before.

He closed his eyes briefly, took a deep breath. 'Okay. What's going on?'

Teagan folded her arms across her chest and glared at him, her breathing calm and controlled despite the hatred she felt for him in that moment. 'You tell me.'

'I'm not psychic, Teagan.'

Keeping her breathing calm and controlled was getting more difficult. She swallowed hard, forced down the hurt. She wouldn't lose her temper with him. She wouldn't yell. Because if she did either of those things there was a very good chance she would cry. And she'd done enough of that.

'We're done, Brendan.'

A fair eyebrow quirked in disbelief. 'Oh, are we, indeed?'

'Yes, we are.'

'And you're not going to tell me why?'

'I don't have to tell you anything.'

'I think you do.'

The anger bubbled. 'You're such a smart guy, you work it out for yourself.'

Standing a little taller, he looked her straight in the eye and opened his mouth to speak.

But in the same way she had when it had been a mistake for members of his family to pause for breath a couple of days before, Teagan took the momentary advantage to talk over him. 'You've been so very clever about helping me figure out all the great wrongs in my life, so why don't you just take a real good, long look at your own? I may have been shut off, Brendan, but when I was shut off the one thing I did do was never risk hurting someone else. Which is something you haven't quite managed, is it? All you've done is prove to me that I was right in the first place. I should never have got involved with you again.'

She tried to end her statement by slamming the door in his face. But he was quick. His hand thudded hard against the wood and he pushed it back, stepping through her doorway with a look of complete determination written all over his face.

'Oh, no, you don't.'

Teagan backed away from him, her fragile hold on her anger rapidly disappearing. 'Get out of my house!'

'No.' He kept walking towards her, pausing only to kick the door closed behind him. 'I think we both know you know me better than that. I'm not going anywhere. Damn it, Teagan, tell me what's going on!'

'You want to know?' She yelled the words at him, stopping her backtracking to glare at him with angry eyes. 'You want to know what's going on?'

'Yes!'

'Fine. Then I'll tell you exactly what's going on!'

He stood stock still as she threw words at him. 'I won't be some rebound affair for you after your ex-wife. That's what's going on!'

CHAPTER SIXTEEN

'REBOUND affair?' He stared at her in astonishment. Where in hell had she got *that* one from? He had known when he'd met Eimear that afternoon that she would most likely mention it—had even told himself that by coming across to explain it to Teagan over pizza straight away he would stop it being a problem. But he hadn't expected her to come to the conclusion she had. 'What in hell are you talking about? You're not a rebound affair!'

'That's exactly what I am.' She stepped towards him again. 'It all makes perfect sense now.'

'Then maybe you should try explaining it to me, because from where I'm standing it doesn't make any sense at all.'

Her arms folded again. 'Are you going to tell me you *didn't* see Rebecca today?'

'No, I'm not going to tell you that. And if you'd waited about ten minutes I'd have told you myself.'

'Just bumped into her, did you?'

'No. I see a fair bit of her, as it happens.'

'Well, isn't that nice for you both?' She smirked up at him. 'Though it would have been nice if you'd *mentioned that before!*'

'Teagan, we never talked about it before.' He shook his

head in frustration and walked across to stand in front of her mantelpiece, setting the pizza box and the wine down along the way.

There was a brief second of charged silence while she waited for him to face her again. 'Because every time I tried talking to you about her you'd shut me out.'

'Are you even going to listen to what I have to say about this, or are you just going to yell at me the whole time?'

She jerked back. Then the cold look came back to her eyes. 'Fine, then.' She moved around an armchair and sat down, carefully smoothing her jeans and then calmly folding her hands onto her lap before she looked up at him. 'Go right ahead. I'm fascinated.'

One long finger waggled in her direction. 'Don't do that.'

'Do what?' She blinked. 'I thought you wanted me to listen?'

Brendan swore and paced away from the mantelpiece, swinging to look at her when he turned around at the sofa. 'You're not going to be open-minded enough to listen when you've already shut yourself off the way you were before.' He paced forward again and stopped in front of her. 'Take a minute and look at everything that has happened between you and me these last few weeks, and then ask yourself if it was all some big lie.'

Her lips pursed tightly before she spoke in an icily controlled tone. 'It's why you wouldn't make love to me. You couldn't. Because you're still in love with her.'

'I am *not* still in love with her! I *work* with her! I do the websites for the company we both worked for. And, as it happens, I *also* work with her husband!'

The word 'husband' widened her eyes.

Brendan smiled a cold smile. 'Didn't expect that one, did you? Knocks your great theory right on the head.'

When her eyes blinked for several minutes he softened, believing he was getting through to her. But then she exasperated him more by calmly stating, 'It doesn't stop me from being a rebound for you. Because, whether she's married or not, you still care about her. I should have known that the minute you changed when I asked about her at the wedding.'

'Yes, I still care about her, Teagan.'

She turned her head away from him.

His voice went flat. 'As a friend. Though how we managed that after everything still stuns me. And you are right about one thing. I *did* change when we talked about her at the wedding.'

Teagan unfolded her hands and used her palms on the arms of the chair to push herself upright again. 'I've heard enough.'

'No, you haven't.' He stepped in and used his large hands on her shoulders, to push her firmly back into the chair. Then he hunched down in front of her, his eyes fixing on hers, demanding she pay attention. 'I changed when we talked about her because I suddenly realised the reason why our marriage didn't work—'

'And you went today to try and explain that to her? I'm sure her new husband would just love that.'

'If she'd wanted him to hear it then I'd have told him too. But I talked to her on her own because there were things I needed to tell her so that she could understand that what happened wasn't her fault. It was mine. And it took being with you again for me to see that.'

A part of her ached at his words. Wanted to know what it was she'd said to him at the wedding that had given him such a clear vision of what had been wrong in his marriage. But when she tried to search her memory for the words she couldn't find them beyond the wall of pain she now felt.

She wanted him to leave. She didn't want to hear about his relationship with someone else. Someone else he had loved and shared his life with that hadn't been her.

How could she ever get past the sense of betrayal she felt after this? And it wasn't even a sense of betrayal because he had cheated on her in some way. It was the betrayal of her trust in him. He had made her believe. Had made her think that with time it would be possible for her to have a deep and meaningful relationship with him that wouldn't be fraught with the same issues her parents had had.

'You know something, Brendan?' She leaned towards him, her voice low. 'I spent years of my life listening to two people have arguments like this one. Not on the same subject. But it basically came down to the same kind of thing. Their relationship didn't work any more than this one ever will. There was never room for a supposedly magical thing like love, because all the rows ever did was kill it stone-dead.'

Thick lashes blinked as he stared at her in silence.

'I used to hear them at night. I would lie in my bed and listen while they tore each other apart with explanations and excuses and reasoning. And then during the day I'd live with two people who had had their hearts broken by so many angry words that they shut themselves off and just existed. Even when they would hug their own children they couldn't put any real love into it. Because that part of their souls had died.'

His jaw worked, and the muscles in his neck moved as he swallowed hard.

'That's what people who care do to each other. And that's why I swore I'd never care that much.'

His eyes flickered as he put what she was saying together. 'And you care that much now?'

Green eyes stared at him, devoid of emotion. And Brendan knew he'd lost.

He pushed himself upright again and stepped back as she got up off the chair. Then he returned to the mantelpiece, his back to her, as she walked further away from him.

'Teagan.' Her name was almost a plea.

She stopped, but didn't turn around.

'If this is it for us, then you need the whole story. That way neither of us can ever use this as an excuse to mess up the rest of our lives.'

Raising his head, he looked at the reflection of her back in the mirror above the mantel. She didn't move, so he started to talk in a low, husky voice. Not caring if she could hear the emotion there. 'You asked me at the wedding if I had been very much in love with Rebecca.'

'That's when you started to change.' In comparison to his voice, hers was still emotionless.

'Yes, because you made me think about it. I only ever wanted to give you honest answers. Because that's the way I wanted it to be with us.'

'I *was* honest with you.'

'Yes, you were. No matter how tough it was for you to do.' He took a breath. 'And that made my answers all the more important. It made me think things through more thoroughly than I might have done before.'

'You told me I thought too much.'

'Yes, and I still think you do that. But I also think *I* didn't think enough. Until I met you again.'

'And what conclusion did you come to?'

'I told you that I didn't think I'd loved her enough, and that was the truth. I think I'd known that all along. What I didn't know was why.'

Teagan's head turned slightly, and she glanced briefly

at his back. 'If you didn't love her enough, then why did you marry her?'

'It was what I wanted. I wanted a wife and a family. You knew that about me. And when I met Rebecca, we got along. We were friends, had work in common, and we just sort of—' he shrugged '—fell into it, I guess. Neither of us took the time to look at it too deeply. When we'd dated a couple of years it made sense to get engaged. When we'd been engaged a couple of years it made sense to get married. But by the time we found out that what we had wasn't strong enough for us to build a family on, we both realised that what we'd been all along was better friends than husband and wife. It took Rebecca meeting Declan for her to know that, and even then she tried to work it out with me. But, rather than fighting to save the marriage, I let her go.'

'And that still hurts?'

'It did.' He glanced at her reflection again, then dropped his gaze to the mantel, frowning. 'But it hurt more because she accused me the whole time of not caring enough, of never having felt the real thing for her, like I'd held a part of myself back. And I kept telling her she was wrong. It wasn't me that was leaving so it wasn't my fault. She wasn't wrong. I didn't know that until you made me think about it. And that's why I had to see her. To tell her I was sorry and that she was right. I *had* held back from her. It wasn't all her fault.'

With his head still bowed he didn't see Teagan's shoulder start to turn. Didn't notice that she was looking directly at him again with questions in her eyes. It took the crackle in her voice when she spoke for him to raise his head and look. 'What did being with me do to make you understand that?'

Dark blue eyes locked with green in the reflection of the mirror. 'You're wrong about being my rebound from Rebecca, Teagan. *Very* wrong.'

She watched as he turned around and walked towards her, stopping a safe distance away. 'How can you be so sure?'

'Because it took being with you again for me to realise how much I love you.'

Her eyes shimmered.

'And to admit to myself how much I loved you when I was twenty-two.'

She blinked while her eyes filled with the tears she'd sworn she wouldn't shed.

'I never knew how much.'

They started to overflow, and the moisture gathered on her lower lashes.

He smiled sadly. 'You aren't my rebound from Rebecca. Rebecca was my rebound from you.' His voice cracked and he stopped to clear his throat, looking away from her face. 'I should never have put her through that. And I couldn't keep pushing you to try and heal from years of pain when I still had to live with knowing what I'd done to her. So I went today to try and fix it. Or at least to leave us both with a clean slate.'

A shaky breath dislodged the tears from her lashes and they streaked, unchecked, down her cheeks.

'And she's happy, you know.' He nodded as he looked towards the door. 'They're expecting their first baby in six months, and they're crazy about each other. What they have is the real deal.'

The first tears gathered on her jaw-line and hung there for a brief second before they dropped silently to the floor.

'When I saw her today the first thing that entered my head was how beautiful you'd be with a baby inside you.

I even allowed myself to hope for a minute that if I was patient enough one day it might happen for us.'

A sob escaped.

'But the truth is, if I'd told you any of this, this early on, you'd have run again. And I couldn't take that chance.' He cleared his throat a second time and managed to look at her for a brief second, his eyes following the path of the tears along her cheeks. 'And it *would* have been too soon for you, Teagan, wouldn't it?'

Even as another sob escaped and the tears flowed freely, Teagan was silently nodding her head. He was right. So, so right. It would have scared the life out of her. Even if she hadn't been given a glimpse of the kind of painful argument that had reminded her of how it could tear two people apart.

Brendan nodded slowly, lifted his hands and pushed them firmly into the pockets of his jeans. 'I thought so.'

Her chest shuddered as she breathed in and out and the realisation of what was happening finally hit her. He was saying goodbye.

His gaze went to the door again and he moved, turning in the direction required to get his feet there. 'At least you know now.'

In the space of two strides he was at the door. And Teagan watched with rapidly blinking eyes as he pulled it open and then gently clicked it closed behind him. And she let him go.

She let him go.

CHAPTER SEVENTEEN

IT WAS raining.

Not that it was an unusual phenomenon for Ireland in the summer. But it had started softly raining the night that Brendan left her house. And it just didn't stop. Like a natural reflection of how Teagan felt.

The irony was that for the first time in her life she could understand better why her parents had been the way they had. And she could almost forgive them for a lot if they had felt as bad as she felt now.

If Brendan had thought she was cut off emotionally before, then he hadn't had a clue how cut off she could actually be. It was like being a shadow. Nature had to make up for the tears she didn't have left.

She was getting through her days somehow. Not enjoying them, or gathering any real memories of what she had done or who she had talked to to fill the time. But she was getting through.

It was the nights that were the worst.

Because at night she was truly alone. And when she sat in her house as the light faded outside, and she couldn't gather the energy to get up to pull the curtains or switch on some lamps, she would look across at his house. And she would ache as she'd never ached before.

And the rain would fall in streaks along the windowpane so that there were always tears before her eyes. Even when she didn't shed them.

Sometimes she would think she could see him, moving around inside his house. She would press her face closer to the glass, holding her breath so she wouldn't fog it up, and she would look for movement. Just a glimpse would do.

But it was as if he was a ghost.

After a few days her phone had started ringing in the evenings. But she ignored it. Thanks to the rain she could even manage to avoid speaking to her other neighbours when, at the end of a work day, they would park in their driveways at the same time and hurry indoors under an umbrella.

When she continued to avoid the phone at home, Eimear started ringing her in work. But she always got the receptionist to say she was busy, or in a conference, or out for lunch.

At the end of a week of calls Eimear appeared at her door. And Teagan realised she couldn't hide for ever.

'I've been trying to get you on the phone for ages.' She pushed past her to get out of the rain and looked around her as she shook moisture from her hair. 'Why are you sitting in the dark?'

Teagan let a lie flow out in answer. 'I'm not long in.'

'I wasn't even sure you were home when I drove up.' Eimear found a lamp on a nearby table and flicked it on, turning to look at her sister. 'Oh, my God. What's wrong?'

Teagan's eyes squinted in the light. 'Could you pull the curtains?'

Eimear stared at her where she was hiding at the side of the window. 'You look dreadful.'

'The curtains.' She waved a hand at them. 'Please, Eimear.'

Stepping over to the large window, she hauled the

curtains across and then swung again to stare at Teagan. 'What's happened?'

'Can we not do this now?'

'No, we *are* doing this now. I thought I was being paranoid when it felt like you were avoiding my calls, but I wasn't, was I?'

'I just need a little time alone.'

'Why?'

Teagan shook her head and walked past her into the kitchen, slightly more confident to move with the curtains drawn. 'I'm just working through some things, that's all.'

'Well, then, let me help.'

It was a reversal of roles. She was acutely aware of that much. And she did appreciate the fact that they were now close enough for Eimear to try to help. But there wasn't any help to be given in this situation. Forcing a smile on her face, she glanced at Eimear while she filled the kettle and plugged it in. 'I just need a little time. Honestly, I'll be fine.'

By the time she'd got mugs from the cupboard Eimear was by her side and had an arm around her shoulders. Teagan stiffened at the contact.

'Teagan, you have been there for me my whole life. Just once let me do the same for you.'

She shook her head. 'I appreciate it, Eimear, I really do. But you can't help.'

'It's Brendan, isn't it?'

'Yes.' The word came out on a monotone. Then she forced another smile, tapping her sister's hand where it lay on her shoulder before stepping out of her hold. 'But you can't help.'

'Did that scumbag break your heart?'

'He's not a scumbag.'

'But he has broken your heart?'

'I broke my own heart.'

There was a gasp from her side. 'You sent him away, didn't you?'

'Eimear—'

'Does he love you?'

She frowned as she looked down at the mugs in her hands. That question she could at least answer with complete conviction. 'Yes, I really believe he does.'

'And you love him, right?'

'Yes.'

The whispered word brought Eimear back to her side. She leaned her head down so she could look into Teagan's eyes. 'Then what went wrong?'

'We'd tear each other apart trying to understand the answer to that. Would probably even fling stuff at each other to find out who's to blame, like Mum and Dad used to.' She looked over at her. 'We already did, thanks to me.'

'Oh, Teagan.' Eimear's eyes immediately filled with tears.

Teagan jumped back from her as if she'd been burned. She couldn't look at someone else crying. Especially not Eimear. 'You should go. Really, I just need some time. It'll be fine.'

'Will it?' Her head shook. 'I don't think it will. Not when it's this big. Something this big a deal isn't exactly an everyday occurrence for you.'

It hadn't been an *any* day occurrence for her. Until Brendan. And everything just kept coming back to him, didn't it? Because the truth was he wasn't the only one who had been in love the first time around. It hadn't taken long for her to figure that one out.

'Can't you fix it with him?'

'I don't know.'

'You stupid idiot!'

The raised voice shocked her. She blinked across the

room with wide eyes. 'You're going to yell at me? That's just terrific—exactly what I need about now!'

'If he loves you, and you love him, and you're not over there trying to fix it—' Eimear pointed at the windows '—then you're a stupid idiot!'

Teagan gaped at her.

'You of all people know how rare something like that is. But instead of fighting for it you're over here, hiding from the world and shutting him out. Do you want to be like this for the rest of your life?'

Teagan blinked dry eyes.

'Fine, then. Go ahead.' She stormed past her and through the living room. 'Be like our parents were. But I'm not going to watch it, Teagan—you hear me?'

'Eimear—'

She stopped, swung on her heel and stormed back, pointing a finger at Teagan's still form. 'Mum and Dad only had themselves to blame for the way they lived their lives, you know. It took me years to understand that. They could have just gone their separate ways and tried to find happiness somewhere else. But they didn't. They *chose* to be miserable and to forget what love was supposed to feel like. Why should you and me allow our lives to be affected by that?'

'They must have thought that once they were married they had to stay married. People believed stuff like that back then. It was just the time, that's all.'

'That's a load of bull. They were too chicken to try, and that's that. It took you yelling at me in a hospital room for me to see I was ruining my chance at happiness because of the legacy they left. And if my yelling at you now is what it takes to make you see the same thing, then I'm going to come over here and yell at you every single day!'

When Eimear stopped, Teagan found herself smiling a

more genuine, if somewhat bittersweet smile. '*Wow*. Who died and made *you* the sensible one?'

'You did, apparently.' She scowled, took a couple of breaths, and then smiled back ruefully. 'Didn't know I had it in me, actually.'

'You're *bossy*.'

'I get that from you.'

Still smiling, Teagan blinked and glanced over at the windows. 'I don't want to be without him, Eimear. I know that. I knew it when I watched him walk out the door. I just don't know how to fix it, that's all.'

'Well, then, you'll just have to find a way.'

'It's not easy.'

'Teagan, nothing worth having ever is. Wait 'til you try childbirth.'

It was as well he wasn't too attached to his house, wasn't it? Because Brendan knew he was going to have to sell it now.

What else was he supposed to do? Live across the road from Teagan, looking for her every day? He might as well sit in his damned home office and stick needles in his eyes.

He just missed her so much.

He missed seeing her dimples appear when she laughed. He missed the way her eyes would sparkle when they argued. He missed the small noises she made when he would touch her and kiss her. But most of all he missed the way he felt when he was with her.

When he had known that he wanted a family of his own some day, and someone to love that could love him back, he had never actually sat down to think what loving them would feel like. Yes, he'd hoped for a partnership, for passion and sharing. But he'd never expected that he would feel like half of a whole without her.

It was what had been missing in his relationship with Rebecca. He had never ached for her the way he ached for Teagan.

When he had talked to Rebecca she had said something that hadn't completely made sense to him. She had told him that with Declan it had never been a case of imagining him in her life for ever that had convinced her he was right for her. It had been imagining what her life would be *without* him that had been the clincher.

And Brendan knew exactly what she meant by that. *Now.*

He lay in bed alone at night and tried to find every solution he could to where they were now. But the one simple fact that stopped every great plan he made dead in the water was that he couldn't do it alone. If Teagan wouldn't take a chance on them then he couldn't force her to. No matter how much he wanted to try. No matter how much he burned to *fight* for it.

It would take both of them to work at it every damn day. That was how it was supposed to be. Years of trying to make it work single-handed would probably do to him a version of what it had done to her parents.

So, much as it killed him, he started to make other plans. Plans that would take him away from her so he couldn't obsess. Because obsessing he was.

It had started out with watching her car pull into her drive in the evening. He would sit with his blinds half drawn, only the light from his computer screen in the room, and he would watch. Would watch as she hid under an umbrella and walked swiftly into her house with her head bowed. Would watch as she moved inside in the shadows and would strain his eyes to see if she was looking out. He would curse her for not putting on a light so he could tell where she was. And he would worry that she was there in the darkness alone, feeling lonely like he was.

In his lowest moments he would even will her to see what was right across the road from her. As if by willing it he could get her to come to him.

But she didn't.

So he got angry. After all, he was back doing exactly what he'd been doing when he'd moved in. Watching and waiting. And it was truly pathetic.

He wasn't going to do it to himself any more.

CHAPTER EIGHTEEN

THE sign went up on the Tuesday, while Teagan was at work. So the first time she saw it was through her rain-splattered windscreen when she turned into the street.

Her headlights hit it, bouncing bright light off the shiny white lettering. FOR SALE.

When she had her car parked in the driveway she just sat there. Looking at the sign in her rearview mirror. He was selling his house. He was leaving for good.

She dragged her eyes away from the mirror, gathered her bag and paperwork from the passenger seat and got out. She juggled everything while she locked the door, then her eyes strayed back to the sign again.

He was *leaving*.

She looked over her shoulder at it again while she juggled once more, opening her front door. And again when she was inside, and was hesitating in closing the door.

She didn't want him to leave. At least while he was across the street she had time to try and find a solution. If he moved away it would make it even tougher than it already was.

She needed a plan *right now*.

Closing the door, she set her belongings onto a side table and wandered aimlessly up the stairs to change out of her damp trouser suit. Automatic pilot took her through the motions. But her mind wasn't on the task.

It was just that she'd never had to fight to keep someone before, and she really didn't know how to go about it. What did other people do? What did they say to convince the person they loved to stay for ever?

Automatic pilot also took her through pulling on jeans and a sweater. It helped her pull trainers onto her feet. Then it took her back downstairs to her darkened living room.

Force of recent habit stopped her from turning on a lamp while she stood in front of the window and stared at the sign.

Then her eyes were distracted as another set of headlights appeared, and Brendan's car pulled into his driveway.

They'd put up the sign.

His eyes caught sight of it when his headlights hit the white lettering. They had said it would be up some time that week, so it wasn't as if he hadn't been expecting it. But somehow seeing it there made everything very final.

He tugged the handbrake into place and lifted his laptop case from the passenger seat. Outside of the car he stared at it while he pushed the automatic lock for the car doors and heard them click shut.

That was that, then. No going back. No more looking across the street and aching.

His eyes flickered towards her house and he scowled. It was about bloody time he started training himself not to do that any more. After all, he had to get used to it, didn't he?

The light rain falling on his head became more persistent, and he shrugged his shoulders beneath his jacket. He should change, really. His body was stiff and sore from driving so much. But the best way he'd found to stop obsessing the last couple of days had been to get around to as many of his clients as possible. Away from the house. No matter how far away they were. And that particular day they had been *miles* away.

With a determined scowl he turned on his heel and walked inside, setting his laptop at the bottom of the stairs before he went to change.

Ten minutes later he lifted it again as he came back down and headed for his office. He didn't let himself even glance towards the window as he flicked on the light switch and unpacked the laptop to load his days work onto the other computer.

Until the house was sold he was going to pretend she wasn't there. So close by and a million miles from where they could have been.

She waited by the window when he got out of the car. Watched him look at the sign and followed him with her eyes when he went inside.

And she felt a sudden sense of urgency.

Words. She needed the right words. This time she wouldn't go and talk to him unprepared, like the night she had gone to his hotel room. This time she would do it right. She had to convince him to stay.

But while she tried to rehearse different ways of saying three small words a light came on across the street. And she could see him.

Her breath caught. Seeing him from a distance wasn't enough.

The laptop hummed as it passed information to the other computer. Hunched over it from a standing position, Brendan did his best to make it the centre of his attention. He knew if he sat down he would swing his office chair back and forth while he waited. And if he did that he'd look out of the window.

And he wasn't going to look out of the window. Even though his traitorous peripheral vision had already noted the fact that his blinds weren't drawn.

Teagan put out a hand to the lamp beside her, her eyes still on Brendan. She moved her arm back and forth while she searched for it, then her fingertips touched the shade and she reached down.

And switched it on.

His peripheral vision caught sight of the light. And for a second he almost looked, his heart thudding a little harder. She hadn't turned a light on for ages. Certainly not with the curtains open, so he could see anything.

He leaned back from the laptop. Stood tall and stared straight ahead at the wall. Then he turned and looked at the cord that would close the blinds.

But as he stepped towards it and reached his arm forward he made the mistake of glancing out. And he saw her. Standing there in the middle of the large window. Staring across at him.

He had seen her. For a minute she thought he would simply close the blind and close her out. And if he did that it would feel like another rejection. One that would set her back.

But while he simply stood and stared back at her she felt an overwhelming sense of hope.

So, with her eyes still locked on his figure, she stepped sidewards, reached out her hand and turned on the light outside her door.

* * *

Their matching doors opened at the same time. Then, regardless of the rain, they walked towards each other. And met halfway, in the middle of the street.

Teagan looked up at him, her heart thundering in her chest. Was he even taller than she remembered? Had he looked so tired the last time she saw him?

She willed herself to say any of the words she'd rehearsed. But she couldn't seem to get beyond the fact that he was there. Right in front of her.

He blinked down at her for long moments, rain soaking through his long sleeved T-shirt, and then simply said, 'Hi,' in a soft, deep voice that tugged at her heart.

'Hi.' Her answer was slightly breathless. She glanced away from his face for a brief second, shrugging one shoulder as she pointed. 'I saw the sign.'

'Yeah.' He forced his eyes away from her face and glanced over his shoulder. 'They said it would go up this week.'

'Are you moving far?'

Broad shoulders shrugged. 'It seemed like a good idea.'

Her breath caught while her eyes stayed fixed on his profile. She blinked off the rain that was beginning to stick to her lashes. 'Because of me?'

'No.' His mouth curved into a small smile at the half-lie. 'Because of me.'

Teagan didn't understand. 'I don't understand.'

'It's not good for my health, living so close to you. One of us is going to have to be brave enough to move.' The small smile was still there when he looked back at her, even if it didn't make it all the way to his dark eyes. 'Last in, first out.'

The attempt at humour washed over her unheeded as she shook her head. 'Brendan—'

'It's all right. Don't worry about it. It just makes more sense.' He was damned if he would stand in the middle of the street and become an object for her sympathy. His chin rose defensively. 'This way we can both get on with our lives.'

His feet made a slight turn, indicating his intention to walk away. But Teagan had already let him walk away once, and she wasn't about to let it happen again. Regardless of how the rain had started to fall heavier on her face, she stepped closer to him. 'Brendan, wait.'

The softly spoken plea stopped him dead. His heart even forgot to beat, knocking itself out of rhythm. But he didn't allow himself to look at her. Looking at her so close for as long as he had had already been rough enough.

'Don't go.'

The words were so soft he barely heard them. Maybe he had wished them said and they hadn't been said at all.

'I don't want you to move away. *Stay.*'

This time they were slightly louder words, and firmer. She had definitely said them. So he had to risk a look, to see what he could read on her face.

She had her head tilted back to look up at him. But it was difficult to tell through the rain and the dim light if the shimmer in her eyes was what he hoped it might be.

And even though his pride wouldn't have allowed him to ask her, his heart needed to know. 'Why?'

Her laughter came out on a shaky note. 'This is so much harder than I thought it would be.'

Pushing his hands into the pockets of his jeans to stop himself from reaching towards her, he simply asked again. 'Why?'

'Because I've never actually told a man that I love him before. That's why.'

Brendan's heart leapt, but he stifled a smile. This had to be right this time. He wouldn't take a chance on saying the wrong thing or starting yet another row.

'Why don't you walk me through it, then?'

Green eyes widened with surprise at the calm response. She didn't know what she'd expected. But surely she could have expected something? A small smile, maybe? A softening of his stance? Anything that might have indicated he was happy to hear her say the words out loud.

'That isn't enough?'

'You tell me.'

'Damn it!' Flinging an arm to one side, she jerked her thumb at the house behind her. 'I've been sitting at the window in that house for over a week now, trying to figure out how to make this better, and now that I'm out here telling you how I feel it isn't enough for you?'

So much for not starting a row. But she wasn't the only one who had had a week of torture in front of a window to endure. 'You think I haven't been doing the same damn thing?'

'Then why are we arguing right now?'

'Because *you* just raised your voice!'

'Then how do I *have* to say it to you to make you believe me?'

It was the way her voice cracked on the words that made him really believe. The glimmer of hope grew in his chest as his voice dropped. 'Try again. We have to get it right this time.'

He was right. They had both done things wrong in the past. Now it was time to take a moment and just tell the truth, the whole truth and nothing but.

'You told me once that the scariest thing about trying for something amazing is the fact that I have to let go.' She stamped her foot in frustration as tears appeared for the millionth time. 'Damn it, and now I'm crying again! I'm getting really, really sick of crying around you.'

'Keep going. You're doing just fine.'

She took a huge breath and forged ahead. 'The truth is I *am* scared. I'm really scared to death. But not of letting go, because I think I started doing that before fear had time to kick in.' Another breath. 'What I'm scared of is losing you. Again. Even though the last time was my own stupid fault.'

Brendan leaned his head down, raising his eyebrows to look her in the eyes. 'Meaning the time you ran?'

A nod, and her voice dropped. 'Meaning the time I ran. I was twenty-one. Is anyone really ready for something this big at twenty-one?'

It was an angle he hadn't thought of, and maybe part of his own reason for not recognising how much he'd felt himself back then. He might have been further up the road of belief than her, in that he'd believed in love and the right someone for everyone, but he hadn't been able to see what was right in front of him until years later. So maybe he hadn't been any more ready for it than she had.

'Maybe not. But there's nothing we can do to fix what happened then.'

It was the tiny 'we' word that did it for her. With a small sniffle she set her tears away and smiled, with a little more hope in her eyes. 'You said "we".'

'I did.'

'So there's still a "we"?'

'Teagan, there's always been a "we". And an "us". For me, anyway.'

It was enough to draw her closer, and to bring excitement to her voice. 'For me too. Not that there was a bat's chance of me admitting it, even to myself. Until you came back. There's never been another you for me, Brendan. Even if I had decided to go out into the world and try, whoever I found wouldn't have been you. And I think a lot of the pain

I felt at being lonely all that time wasn't because I was alone. But because you weren't there.'

That was it. He wasn't able to stand still any more. Raising his hands, he framed her rain-soaked face, his thumbs rubbing across her cheeks. 'This stuff doesn't happen every day. Some people spend their whole lives looking and they never find it. That makes us lucky sons-of—'

'Don't you dare.' She smiled up at him. 'I've met your mother.'

He laughed.

She grabbed hold of his wet shirt at his waist, bunched it into her fists and held on tight. 'I *love* you.'

The rain continued to fall on them both as they smiled at each other. But it didn't matter a damn, to either of them. Brendan leaned a little closer, determined to say everything before he kissed her again. Because when he started kissing her he had absolutely no intention of stopping.

'I warn you, Teagan Delaney, this is *it* this time. Once I have you I won't want to let go. Ever. Sitting in that house knowing you were so close was the worst torture I've ever endured, and I can't do it again. I mean it. So you either know that this is for ever and you work with me to keep it, or we both walk away now and pray that it'll stop hurting some time before we die.'

'I don't want you to let go. Ever.' It took only a sway to touch her body along the length of his. Then she tilted her head right back to look at him, blinking the rain from her eyes as she smiled up at him. 'I'm relying on you not to let go. Because I won't. I want to fall asleep with your arms around me every night, and I want to wake up there every morning. I love you. I always have.'

'And I love you. Always have, always will.' He rubbed his thumbs along her cheeks again, smiled at the rain that

ran over her face. Then he rounded his shoulders and
lowered his head 'til his mouth was on hers.

Teagan let out a sigh, untangled her fists and reached
her hands up under his arms until she held his shoulders.
She felt the muscles bunch beneath her fingers, then relax,
felt his chest rise against her breasts and then fall in a
shuddering sigh. And she kissed him back with a week's
worth of pent-up emotion.

He released his hands from her face, groaning as he
deepened the kiss, sought her tongue with his. His arms
circled her and crushed her to him, his hands moving down
her back and then under the hem of her wet sweater, until
his fingers touched cool skin.

Wrenching his mouth from hers, he tilted his head and
began the same assault from a different angle. Then again,
and again. Then again. Over and over, until they were both
breathing hard and soaking wet from the rain that fell.

Hands pulling back from her skin, he moved to her
waist and lifted her off the ground, so high that he had to
tilt his head back to keep kissing her.

Teagan lifted her head and looked down at him,
laughter bubbling from her chest. She'd never been so
completely happy before. Never felt as if she was, quite
literally, floating. Even without his help keeping her feet
off the ground.

And he laughed with her, threw her up an inch, then let
her slide slowly down along the length of him. His voice
was husky with need when he spoke again. 'Just so you
know, this time there's no question about us not making
love. You're mine.'

She knew what he was saying. Knew it and wanted it.
Already she could visualise the next step to all the long and
tortuous sessions of intimacy they'd been practising.

'Then take me.' She challenged him with a sassy lift of her chin. 'Back to your house. I'll show you how much I love you, and you can show me how much you love me.'

'Sweetheart…' He bent down to put an arm behind her knees and swept her up into his arms. 'A lifetime isn't long enough for me to do that.'

Kissing along the side of his neck as he turned and carried her back towards his open doorway, she whispered, 'Slowly. I'd heard that slow was good.'

The rain stopped as they reached the door and they both looked upwards. The last clouds were rolling away and stars peeked out above their heads. As they looked back into each other's faces it was almost as if they both realised the significance of it and knew that the other one knew too.

'Do you believe in fate, Teagan?'

'Now that I've got you I can believe in anything.'

EPILOGUE

IT WAS Christmas chaos. And Teagan was loving every single minute of it.

'Isn't this just the best Christmas you ever remember having?' Eimear plunked herself down on the large sofa at Teagan's side. 'It's as well Brendan's folks have such a massive house, I tell you. How many of them *are* there, exactly? I've lost count.'

Teagan laughed. 'About ninety when you add us, I think. The kids are loving it, though.'

There was a stream of them running around. Teagan's nephew and nieces mixed with seven other nieces and nephews of Brendan's. And at the back of the running stream of children was Meghan, trying her absolute best to keep up with legs that hadn't completely got the hang of it, and earning affectionate laughter when she always arrived five minutes behind the rest.

'You'll have to do something about adding to the numbers some time soon.'

Teagan blushed. 'Oh, we're working on it.'

'Careful, now, kids. Watch someone doesn't fall over something.' Louisa waved a massive platter of turkey sandwiches under their noses with a beaming smile. 'I swear it'll take a year to recover from all the mess. Isn't it lovely? I'm so glad you could all come. Wouldn't have been the same without you here. House is like a library these days, with everyone moving out. Thank goodness I have the last two wee ones still at home. Don't know what I'll do when they leave.'

She waved the platter until they took a sandwich each. Teagan grinned as she looked over at the 'last two wee ones', where they stood by Brendan in front of the fire-place. 'Wee' was probably the last word she would have used to describe his younger brothers, both of them easily the same height.

'You'll have to take all the grandchildren on different weekends, Mrs McNamara.' Eimear smiled up at her. 'That'll soon have you looking for a rest.'

'Oh, you can never have enough grandchildren, darling. And I keep telling you—' she swatted her with a teatowel '—it's Louisa. You'll have to bring your three round more often after this. Why, we're all one big happy family here. And maybe you could take the time to persuade this sister of yours to explain to Brendan how to get us some more little ones. You'd have thought they'd have read a book or something by now.'

Eimear laughed loudly. 'You'd have thought.' Then she aimed a wink in Teagan's direction.

'Took Cormac and myself about five minutes to work it out.' Louisa leaned close to give an exaggerated wink and hiss loudly, 'Still remember how, after all these years.'

'And on that note…' Teagan gave Eimear her sandwich and stood up, her eyes seeking out Brendan. 'I think I'll go have a talk to Brendan.'

His gaze fell on her as she rose and placed a kiss on his mother's cheek. It was something they did automatically after five months together—an almost silent radar that knew where the other one was without having to search. And she smiled back when he smiled over at her.

He raised his brows in question, and she jerked her head in the direction of the door. They were pretty damn good at silent communication too. In oh, so many ways.

It took them a while to make their way through the room—presents to admire with their new owners, hugs to give and receive, jokes to be laughed at. But eventually, their hands joined, they ran for the safety of the empty dining room.

Then his mouth was on hers, for a long kiss that stole the breath from her lungs.

When his head finally rose he grinned down at her. 'I remember you.'

'It's been a while.' She leaned back against the circle of his arms. 'Miss me?'

'Always.' He kissed her again.

'I have something for you.'

His eyes twinkled as she whispered the words against his lips. 'I bet you do. I have something for *you* too.'

She laughed, and kissed him soundly. 'That's not what I meant.'

The comment was met with an innocent blinking of his lashes. 'Why, Teagan, I'm shocked. That's not what *I* meant either.'

Another long kiss, then he whispered in her ear, 'Though I *do* have that for you later,' before he loosened his arms, retook her hand and tugged her past the long table to the windows at the other end of the room.

When he stopped he let go of her hand and put both hands on her shoulders to turn her to face him. Then he let go again and stood back a step. 'This seems like the right place.'

She blinked in confusion as he smiled a potent smile at her and slowly let his eyes rise upwards. Following his gaze, she felt her heart catch, and she gasped, 'Mistletoe.'

Brendan waited until her eyes met his again. 'Mistletoe.'

It was the most romantic thing. Teagan officially *loved* mistletoe.

Reaching into his pocket, he produced a small wrapped box and placed it into her hand, his eyes on her fingers as he closed them around it. He cleared his throat. 'I would have done this much sooner, just so you know. But at the start I thought I'd give you a chance to see we were working out. Then we went and decided to get a house together and had all that moving stuff to do. And then Christmas just seemed like a romantic kind of a time.' He shrugged. 'For us, anyway.'

Teagan's eyes flickered over the blond spiking hair on his head, her heart swelling. She would never in a million years have believed she could love him more than she already did. *'Yes.'*

His head rose, his eyes dancing at her. 'I haven't asked you yet.'

'It's still a yes. You know it's a yes. We were always going to do this. I didn't think there was any question.'

'Don't you want me to say the words?'

Stepping closer, so that her body lined up with his, she tilted her head back, her voice low. 'I don't need the words. I see what I need every day in your eyes. You love me. I love you. We've been married for months in every way that matters. We just haven't fitted in a ceremony. So the answer is yes.' She smiled. 'It's been yes since the day your sister got married.'

He hadn't known that, and he loved that he still got to discover new things about her. 'For me too.'

The kiss was tender, slow and deliberate. But as Teagan's fingers closed around the box in her hand she felt a niggle at the back of her mind. There was something else, wasn't there? He was just so damn good at distracting her with his kisses...

Then she remembered, and pulled her mouth free. 'Oh, no.'

Brendan laughed at her petulent tone, his breath fanning over her swollen lips. 'Well, of all the things you've said when I've kissed you, I have to say that's the most original.'

'You kind of ruined *my* surprise, that's all.'

'Well, hell—shoot me for asking you to spend for ever with me.'

She laughed up at him and batted his arm with her free hand. 'I just had this whole plan of what I was going to say, and you went and beat me to it, that's all. It's been tougher than you know, not saying it before now. But Christmas seemed like a romantic time.'

'*You* were going to propose to *me*?' His eyebrows rose in question.

'Well, I might have thrown that one in somewhere. I didn't rehearse that bit, though.'

'I thought you said you didn't need words?'

He was still a wise guy. And still right. She didn't need words for this one. With the ancient smile women had practised for centuries, she pushed the ring box back into his trouser pocket. 'Hang on to that a minute. I'll need you to put it on a finger for me when we're done.'

His body immediately stiffened until her hand was removed. Then he grinned a wicked grin.

Which made her laugh again.

He let out a long whistle. 'Okay, I'm definitely ready.'

'You're right, you know. There are no words needed for

this one. Though it *was* a pretty speech, just so you know.' Her eyes locked on his, she reached for his wrists, then brought his hands forward and smoothed the palms across her stomach.

His eyes dropped down, looking where his hands rested. His fingers splayed out, his thumbs caressing back and forth over the rounded curve. And then he looked up, his eyes shimmering.

Teagan smiled, her eyes filling with happy tears. Then she laughed, a low, softly female laugh, and said, her voice hoarse, 'Happy Christmas.'

His familiar voice wavered. 'How long have you known?'

'Just a couple of weeks.' She grinned. 'It was kind of inevitable, if you think about it.'

If she had ever had any doubts left about how he felt about her, it was all in his eyes at that moment. Even while his eyes still shimmered he was smiling. 'My mother is going to kill me for not having married you sooner.'

'She can deal with me.' Reaching up, she framed his face with her small hands, her thumbs touching the corners of his mouth. 'I spent all that time on my own, denying what my heart wanted, Brendan.' She stood up on her tiptoes and whispered against his mouth, 'Now I have it all. Now *we* have it all.'

'I love you.'

'I know you do.' She smiled against his mouth. 'Daddy.'

* * * * *

New York Times *bestselling author Linda Lael Miller is back with a new romance featuring the heartwarming McKettrick family from Silhouette Special Edition.*

SIERRA'S HOMECOMING
by Linda Lael Miller

On sale December 2006,
wherever books are sold.

Turn the page for a sneak preview!

Soft, smoky music poured into the room.

The next thing she knew, Sierra was in Travis's arms, close against that chest she'd admired earlier, and they were slow dancing.

Why didn't she pull away?

"Relax," he said. His breath was warm in her hair.

She giggled, more nervous than amused. What was the matter with her? She was attracted to Travis, had been from the first, and he was clearly attracted to her. They were both adults. Why not enjoy a little slow dancing in a ranch-house kitchen?

Because slow dancing led to other things. She took a step back and felt the counter flush against her lower back. Travis naturally came with her, since they were holding hands and he had one arm around her waist.

Simple physics.

Then he kissed her.

Physics again—this time, not so simple.

"Yikes," she said, when their mouths parted.

He grinned. "Nobody's ever said that after I kissed them."

She felt the heat and substance of his body pressed against hers. "It's going to happen, isn't it?" she heard herself whisper.

"Yep," Travis answered.

"But not tonight," Sierra said on a sigh.

"Probably not," Travis agreed.

"When, then?"

He chuckled, gave her a slow, nibbling kiss. "Tomorrow morning," he said. "After you drop Liam off at school."

"Isn't that...a little...soon?"

"Not soon enough," Travis answered, his voice husky. "Not nearly soon enough."

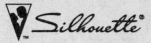

HARLEQUIN® *Romance*®

**From the Heart.
For the Heart.**

Get swept away into the Outback
with two of Harlequin Romance's
top authors.

Coming in December...

Claiming the Cattleman's Heart
BY BARBARA HANNAY

And in January don't miss...

Outback Man Seeks Wife
BY MARGARET WAY

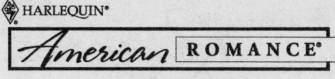

REQUEST YOUR FREE BOOKS!
2 FREE NOVELS PLUS 2
FREE GIFTS!

HARLEQUIN ROMANCE

From the Heart, For the Heart

HR06

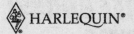

Coming Next Month

#3923 THE BRIDE OF MONTEFALCO Rebecca Winters
By Royal Appointment

Ally Parker has come to Italy with questions about her past that only Gino, duke of the aristocratic Montefalco family, can answer. Swept away to Gino's magical country estate, Ally begins to fall in love with the brooding Italian. But will the secrets and sins of the past keep Gino from making Ally the rightful bride of Montefalco…?

#3924 CRAZY ABOUT THE BOSS Teresa Southwick
The Brides of Bella Lucia

Billionaire Jack Valentine returns to London with his trusted assistant Madison Ford to make or break the Bella Lucia business. Until now, Maddy enjoyed a professional relationship with her boss. But the Jack she knew is nothing like this intoxicating man with fire in his eyes and pain in his soul. Maddy knows she could fall for him—but this Jack could easily break her heart….

#3925 CLAIMING THE CATTLEMAN'S HEART Barbara Hannay

All rugged cattle station owner Daniel Renton wants to do is build a relationship with his motherless daughter. But then newcomer Lily Halliday breezes into town like a breath of fresh air. A bond begins to form between them, but Daniel has to guard his heart and resist. Lily needs to convince Daniel to trust her—because a life with him will be worth the wait!

#3926 INHERITED: BABY Nicola Marsh

Riley Bourke is a single, successful businessman—who knows nothing about children! And Maya Edison is doing just fine on her own; she doesn't need a man to hold her hand…or a part-time father for her son. But as Riley starts to nudge his way into their hearts, Maya gives him an ultimatum: either he's *properly* part of their lives…or there's no place for him at all!